LOOKING FOR A DEAD GUY
The Funny Detective – Volume 4

David Berardelli

LOOKING FOR A DEAD GUY
The Funny Detective – Volume 4

FICTION4ALL

DAY ONE

Chapter 1

At one-thirty in the afternoon, the sun in late June fills the Central Florida sky with blinding neon, forcing motorists and pedestrians to scramble for awnings, beach umbrellas, baseball caps, heavily tinted windows, and polarized sunglasses.

Orange Avenue, loud and just as chaotic as it was two hours earlier, when I'd left my office for an early lunch, remained chaotic with constant bumper-to-bumper traffic.

I usually don't take two hours for lunch, but the morning had dragged on like a half-smashed cockroach. Rather than sit at my desk, waiting for a prospective client to pop on in, I decided to get up for a change of scenery. Besides, I hadn't had much breakfast, and my empty stomach was irritating me even more than my empty office.

Smilin' Susie's, my favorite breakfast eatery, had recently hired a new waitress, who turned out to be a babe. Everyone who knows me will tell you that I've always been a sucker for new babes. Now that I'm thinking about it, even used babes have been known to make me act like a clueless idiot.

This new waitress, however, was hands-off. The sad fact was that she truly *was* a babe, with everything going for her—long, flowing blond hair, big blue eyes, dimples, and a body with enough curves to make any guy lose his equilibrium. Her calves looked great in spite of the white orthopedic shoes she wore. To make matters worse, her name tag said *Miranda*—a name most guys dream about.

Everything about her was sexy, classy, and top of the line.

The deal-breaker was the huge glittering rock she wore on the third finger of her left hand.

In other words, breakfast was great despite the frustration of dealing with a waitress I couldn't even flirt with.

Just one block away, my tiny office, where I run my one-man detective agency, awaited my return. It was normally a three-minute walk. However, on this particular occasion, I knew even before I reached the end of the block that my trip back was going to take slightly longer than three minutes.

A rental car filled with foreigners had stopped abruptly at the curb right in front of me.

It's irritating when a vehicle stops right in front of you, blocking your way. It's also irritating when its passengers are all chattering away loudly at you, and even worse when they're doing it in a foreign language. I've lived in Florida most of my life and have heard just about every known language in the civilized world, but I had no earthly idea where this batch was from. They were all yelling at once--which made this even more frustrating. I couldn't tell anything about them by their clothes--tourists usually dress as if they'd just crawled out of a Goodwill donation box. Both sexes wore tank tops and bright-colored shorts. I also saw giant-rimmed sunglasses beneath their visors and two Mickey Mouse hats. A heavy cloud of B.O. mixed with cigarettes, coffee and cheap aftershave gushed out through the open window.

I knew better than try out my old high school French. Last year, when I was approached by a Frenchman, I tried giving him directions to Disney in French. He immediately stormed off, ranting in his own language, and flipping me the bird. Later that evening, when I consulted Google Translate to check out what I'd really said, I discovered that I'd mispronounced a few words, used the wrong verbs, and put the sentence in the wrong order. I'd actually told him that I wanted to disgrace myself in his pocket.

A few months ago, I tried the same thing with a tourist in his native Spanish. When he tried running me over with his rental, I knew I must have messed up again. Consulting the translate site once again, I found out that I'd told him his sister liked to watch me blow my nose.

Since then, I decided to just listen and see what turned up. When I heard them blurt out a familiar word or two, I quickly discovered that this case would be fairly easy. "*Diss-nee*" was one of the obvious clues. "*Oonee-versai Shtoo-dios*" also clearly suggested the source of their dilemma.

However, the long line of traffic waiting nervously behind them warned me of impending doom, suggesting I handle this problem as quickly as possible. Many of the drivers had already begun tapping their horns and yelling loudly. Since the yelling penetrating the atmosphere was in English, I had no problem understanding. Things were about to get ugly.

The tourists continued chattering away, eager to get to their destination. I'd been in this situation many times before. With most tourists, you don't have to say anything. All you have to do is point. They're usually so excited and in so much of a hurry that they'll zip away long before you've finished trying to help them.

I made a few quick gestures with my hands, pointing straight ahead, toward the south. I then held up three fingers and flicked my right thumb to my right, indicating west.

My instincts quickly proved right-on. The driver grinned and nodded eagerly. They all yelled "*danke!*" and "*merci!*" simultaneously. The driver raised his arm and waved, and another pungent miasma of B.O. swept toward me. The rental car squeaked away from the curb and slipped recklessly through the red light amidst another chorus of angry honking.

Satisfied peace had just been restored, I sighed in relief. Despite the two dozen or so frustrated drivers all caught helplessly at the red light, life could resume.

I stepped down from the curb and crossed the street.

A couple of minutes later, I reached my block. The strip mall buzzed with activity in front of the liquor store one door down, the Chinese restaurant on the far side of the building, and the tee shirt shop on the other side of my office. Only one vehicle was parked in front of my place. That was, of course, my classic black '75 TransAm. As I approached the heavy glass door, the three empty chairs lined up against my storefront window warned me of another quiet, unprofitable afternoon. But as soon as I pulled the door open, I saw that my office wasn't quite empty.

A female with a shock of fiery red hair sat at my desk, watching me curiously.

***

Under normal circumstances, I should have welcomed the intrusion.

After all, I hadn't had a client in two weeks. Coming back from lunch and finding a prospective client in my office should be a good thing. Especially when the prospective client happened to be a cute redhead.

However, this wasn't the case. The cute redhead sitting in my chair was no more than twelve or thirteen years old.

I've never been a great fan of kids. They were always loud and unruly, and walked around angry all the time. I'd never wanted kids and was grateful that my ex-wife Phil never wanted any, either. I hadn't liked being around them since I was a kid myself and saw no fondness for them as I grew older.

It was no wonder that I found it difficult to keep from grabbing her by the scruff of the neck, picking her up and tossing her outside.

Knowing that would most likely get me arrested, I tried staring her down. It worked for some, especially when I used my squinty-eyed, Clint Eastwood technique. However, others just weren't smart enough to get the message. They'd ask if something was wrong with my eyes—or if I needed glasses.

In this case, she stared back at me for a little while. Then she said, "Got something in your eye?"

I decided right then that I should try a more sensible tactic.

"Like some coffee?"

She wrinkled her nose.

"How about a drink?"

She gawked at me as if I were some laboratory experiment that had gone bad. "I'm fourteen."

She obviously didn't catch the irony. I reminded myself that my brilliant wit was oftentimes lost on less gifted individuals. I wasn't surprised in this instance. The last couple of generations had turned out a batch of strange, often clueless individuals who seemed to zone out automatically when dealing with actual people. If you weren't one of their Facebook friends or a name in their address book, they looked at you as if cockroaches were crawling out of your ears.

In any event, she hadn't scored any points with me. And the fact that she was sitting at my desk didn't exactly make me want to add her to my Christmas card list—even if I had one.

"I don't know if you're aware of this, but you're in my seat."

She regarded me curiously, as someone would watch some alien micro-organism swimming around in a test tube. She didn't get up, and I could tell she had no intention of doing so.

I had to convince her I was serious. She was a cute kid, with the biggest blue eyes I'd ever seen. Judging by her thick red hair and pretty face, I was confident she'd turn into a genuine babe in just a couple of years.

But she wasn't a babe right now, and that realization alone brought me to my senses. She was a bratty kid sitting where she shouldn't be sitting and daring me to do something about it.

Whether she knew it or not, she'd come to the wrong place and was showing her butt to the wrong guy. Since I hadn't been able to drum up any business in a while, I was in no mood for bullshit--especially from a skinny midget with big blue eyes, great hair, and a bad attitude.

Even so, I decided to put my frustration aside for the moment and try a more civilized approach. "Like I just said, you're in my seat. I'd really appreciate it if you stopped what you were doing and got out of it."

Still no reply.

"Listen...I don't know what you're doing here, but like I just said--"

"I came to tell you about a possible crime."

Her statement stopped me right in my tracks. That simple explanation hadn't occurred to me. I'd been so focused on her invading my personal space that I never once considered why she'd come here in the first place.

"Really?" I knew that sounded kind of lame, but she'd caught me off-guard, and I found that I was at a loss for words.

"You're a detective, aren'tcha?"

"That's what the sign says on the door…"

Those big blue eyes drifted down my shirt before climbing back up to my face. If she'd been fifteen years older, I would have enjoyed the once-over.

But she *wasn't* fifteen years older--she was a little girl. Someone's daughter. She was just a scrawny little kid barely in high school. I probably had scars older than she was.

It was time to get down to business. I jabbed a thumb at the chair facing the desk. "You really need to be sitting in that chair."

"Why?"

Damn, she was irritating… "Listen…and try to absorb this. This is my office and that's my desk. I might sound a little old-fashioned, but while I'm sitting there, it kind of makes me feel like I'm the one in charge—get it?"

"Isn't the person hiring you the one in charge?"

"You're really pushing my buttons, girl…"

She didn't reply right off, but I could tell she was thinking up a good zinger.

"You really haven't told me the actual reason why you came here, have you?"

"I just said I did. Weren't you listening?"

"Yeah. I had my listening ears on. I even had them plugged in."

"Then why don't you believe me?"

"You've been busting my chops ever since I came back."

"Why? Because I'm sitting in your stupid chair?"

"Yeah, because of that. And by the way, don't say anything bad about my chair. She and I go way back."

"She? Seriously?"

"*He* would sound weird—don't you think?"

She didn't reply. I think I was beginning to confuse her.

"So...now that we've got everything straightened out, you can leave and go find someone else to antagonize."

She crossed her arms over her skinny chest and glared. "Name one reason why you don't believe me."

"You're too young."

"What's that have to do with anything?"

"I don't trust kids."

"Weren't you a kid once?"

"That's why I don't trust them."

"Figures..."

"If you really came here to report a crime, you would've already done it by now. You wouldn't be sitting in my chair, arguing with me..."

"Why else would I be here?" She looked around. "It's not exactly a cool place to be, ya know. You don't have a TV. You don't even have

13

a cold drink or snack machine for someone to use while they wait for you to come back from your super long lunch. And unless you're a dweeb that likes watching traffic, the view isn't exactly first-rate, either."

I wouldn't have believed it possible, but she was getting even more irritating. I began wondering who I'd pissed off lately. It would take much too long to go through the complete list. Pissing off people was what I did, and I did it well. I considered myself an expert. But I wasn't in the mood for this. "I must have pissed off *some*one bad enough for them to send over a bratty kid as a practical joke..."

"You're really cold, Mister..."

"I get that a lot."

She finally got up and circled the desk. She went over to the chair and plopped down. She wasn't quite five feet tall and weighed maybe eighty pounds. She wore faded jeans and a turquoise tank top with a batch of glittering silver stars on the back, and her bushy red hair was tied in a thick ponytail ending a couple of inches below her shoulder blades. A cluster of tiny freckles peppered her cheekbones, but you couldn't see them unless you were really close. She really was pretty. I figured she'd be a knockout in two or three years.

But judging by her manner and her attitude, I didn't think she'd make it.

She shrugged. "Better?"

"I don't feel like doing a cartwheel or breaking out in a chorus of Kumbaya, but yeah,

I'm reasonably satisfied." I sat down and pushed my chair closer. She'd moved my pen and doodle pad a couple of inches from their usual place on the blotter. I didn't like people touching my stuff, but I repositioned them silently, without making nasty faces or even giving her a quick glare.

"You always take two hours for lunch?"

"Listen, kid--"

"It's almost two." She glanced at the clock on the wall to my right. "I got here just after one. I've been waiting ever since."

"I had a slow morning. I needed a change of scenery."

"You should've left a note or something."

Now she was making me feel guilty for being out of the office. I thought once again about tossing her out into the street. This time, I smiled at the image.

"What's so funny?"

No need to tell her what I was thinking.

"Listen. Kid... You need to show a little respect when you talk to grownups."

"I hear that a lot--usually from my dad."

"You should pay attention to him."

"So...where *were* you for two hours?"

"Kid, you're too damned young to be judging people. Once you're old enough to venture out on your own, then you can start your own business and take as long as you like for lunch."

"You could've missed out on other clients while you were gone so long..."

"Kid, don't you have to be anywhere else right now? School, maybe? Boot camp, perhaps?"

"Boot camp?"

"I'm just grasping at straws."

"Why Boot camp?"

"It's where kids go when—"

"I know what it is. I'm not out of control. And school's been out for over a week. And by the way, I'm *Tabby*--not *kid*."

"Is that short for Tabitha?"

"No one calls me that."

"Tabby? Or Tabitha?"

"I just said--"

"Listen...Tabitha--"

"*Tabby*..."

"Whatever. I'm going to ask you this once again, and this time I don't want any bull, all right?"

"You can say bullshit. I've heard it a zillion times before. My dad uses it. My mom, too—especially when she's pissed."

"Watch your language. Just tell me why you're here so you can go. I've got stuff to do."

She watched me for a few moments and frowned. "How old are you?"

"What?"

"They keep telling me people get hard of hearing when they reach a certain age."

"For your information, I've heard every damned word you've said, thank you very much."

"Then why do you keep asking me why I'm here even after I keep telling you why I'm here?"

"Let me say it once more and leave it at that: I don't believe you're here to report a crime."

"But it's true."

16

"You're really here to report a crime?"

"Yeah."

"A *real* crime?"

She sent over another glare. "You mean, did I see a crime actually happen? Or am I imagining it?"

Her directness caught me off-guard. This girl was gonna cause a bunch of problems for a bunch of people when she started out on her own. "I didn't say that, but yeah, that explanation'll do."

"That's why I'm here." A shrug. "Someone could be in trouble, ya know..."

"So?"

"Don't you care if someone's in trouble?"

"In case you haven't noticed, I'm not the one in charge of keeping the world safe. I couldn't even if I wanted to."

"Huh?"

"People get in trouble all the time. They get in trouble everywhere. You can't expect me to care about everyone who might be in trouble..."

"Not even if you think this person could be dead?"

I sat up. "Are you trying to tell me you saw a *murder* being committed?"

"I'm not sure..."

"What *are* you saying?"

"I might have seen some dude being beat up and tossed in the trunk of someone's car."

"Where'd you see this?"

She sat forward. I could see that she was serious; her eyes had grown considerably. I no longer saw her as a bratty kid with an attitude. She'd suddenly become a frightened little girl.

She took a breath. "It happened right across the street from my home."

Chapter 2

My beautiful dead buddy Mike appeared in the room.

Her form was hazy, as usual when she first appeared from the Other Side, but I could see her form-fitting designer jeans, open-toed pumps, and loose-fitting red crop top. This had become her standard outfit--possibly because she knew how much I liked it. Her thick chestnut hair spilled heavily over her shoulders. She knew how much I liked that, as well.

"Is that cute little thing a client?" she asked, her large almond eyes giving the girl the once-over. "Or is this something I really shouldn't know anything about?"

As usual, Mike was playing with me. But it was okay; she and I had been through a lot together. She'd saved my life dozens of times in the last few years and I considered her my very best friend. It didn't matter one bit to me that she was dead. In my world, she was just as real as anyone else I knew.

"A witness to a crime," I mumbled.

"Huh?" The kid was watching me.

"I said you've witnessed a crime." I was talking to Mike but looking at the kid. It wouldn't have been very bright to let her or anyone else know that I communicated daily with a dead babe.

"Does that mean you'll look into this?" the kid asked.

"I'm not sure if this is something I can handle."

"Why not? We could be talking about murder, ya know."

"Maybe…"

"I told you I was serious. I'm not making this up."

"I'm sure you're serious about what you thought you saw."

"*Thought*?" I could tell right off that I'd nudged one of her buttons. "You just said I witnessed a crime. Now you're saying I only *think* I witnessed a crime?"

"I was just talking out loud."

"People do that when they get older, don't they?"

"Ouch." Mike winced.

"One thing you should already know is that when you want someone to do you a favor, you don't insult them first. It doesn't make things any easier, for one thing, and it doesn't give them the incentive needed to do the favor."

The kid looked down at her lap. "Sorry…"

"Now…getting back to business… I can't decide if I'll take the case unless I know specifically what happened."

"I just told you. I saw some dude being tossed in the trunk of someone's car. I told you that a minute ago--remember?"

"Of course I remember."

"You're not acting like you do."

"How am I acting?"

"Well…you look kinda weird."

20

"How is *that* possible?"

"Got a couple of minutes?" Mike asked.

I shot her a glare.

"You keep getting this really freaky look on your face," the kid said. "You're not having a heart attack, are ya?"

Mike blinked. "Is there something you haven't told me? Should I worry?"

I was getting even more annoyed. Now there were *two* of them picking on me.

"I'm not having a damned heart attack…"

"Why'd she mention it, then?" Mike asked.

"She's delusional."

"Huh?"

"I said you're delusional."

The kid frowned. "I guess now you're gonna tell me you don't believe me again…"

"Listen, kid…"

"*Tabby*. Can't you even remember my name?"

"I'm beginning to think I came in at the wrong time." Mike shook her head.

"This isn't funny," I told Mike.

"Does it look like I'm laughing?" The kid sat up. "What's wrong with you? Just 'cause I'm only fourteen, you think I'm busting your chops. Can't you talk to me without treating me like a little kid?"

"You *are* a little kid…"

"I'm practically old enough to drive."

"You're still a little kid."

"That doesn't mean I didn't see something bad happen!" Her face reddened. "What's wrong with you grownups? Did you forget you were a kid once?"

"You're *such* a brute," Mike said.

I felt like I'd just kicked a sick puppy.

"Listen...Tabby...I'm sorry I came off sounding like...well, like such a--"

"Jerk," she threw in. "Asshole. Son of a--"

"Jerk was fine. And you really need to watch your language."

"You should've let her go on," Mike said. "She was letting off steam."

I tossed Mike another quick glare. "Like I said, I'm sorry. And you're right. I really haven't given you a chance to tell me about this. If you'll give me another chance, I promise I'll listen to what you've got to say."

"Really?"

"Really."

Her eyes grew. "You'll really *listen* this time?"

"I said I would. But you've got to tell me everything, all right?"

"Everything?"

"First of all, what's your name?"

She stiffened. "I just told you--"

"Your *full* name. And your address. Then you can tell me about your father and your mother, and finally what you actually saw."

She sat back in the chair. "My name is Tabitha Jane Kendrick, but like I told you before, everyone calls me Tabby."

"Cute," Mike said. "She looks like a Tabby."

I gave her another quick glare.

"Why do you keep doing that?" the kid asked.

"Doing what?"

"You keep looking at something above my head. Then you get this really disgusted look on your face. You freaking out or something?"

"It's something old folks do. Whenever we get confused or angry, we focus on some inanimate object in the room and frown at it. It releases tension and helps us unwind."

"Is *that* what I am to you?" Mike asked. "An inanimate object?"

The kid was watching me again. "Never heard *that* one before…"

"Like I said, it takes the edge off."

"You don't…hear *voices*, do ya?"

"Not all the time. I usually ignore them in mixed company."

Both the kid and Mike stared at me.

After a moment, the kid said, "Anyway, we live on Oak Ridge Road."

"What about your dad and mom?"

"They live there, too."

"That's *not* what I meant."

"My dad's name is Peter, but everyone calls him Pete."

"And your mom?"

"Mom's name is Sharon."

"What's your dad do?"

"He's in Iraq."

"What branch?"

"Marines." She raised a brow. "You're not writing any of this down."

"Despite what you think, I've got a first-class memory. How long's he been there?"

"Been where?"

"In Iraq. Your dad."

"About six months."

"What's your mom do?"

"She works in a bank on the Trail."

"How long?"

"A couple of years."

"What did she do before?"

"She worked in a different bank."

"Where?"

"Kissimmee."

"Your mom's always worked in a bank?"

"Ever since I can remember."

"Tell me what you saw. You said this happened right across the street from your house?"

"I was looking out the window one night and saw this guy come out of our neighbor's house."

"Why were you doing that?"

"Doing what?"

"Looking out the window."

She frowned. "I like looking at the stars before I go to bed. What's wrong with that?"

"You don't have to get huffy…"

"Some of my friends think I'm weird doing that, but I don't care."

"Not a thing wrong with that."

"Really?"

"Really. Now go on…"

"Two other dudes came out of the house, walked right up to him and hit him over the head."

"You saw that?"

"Well, it was dark, but I figured that's what happened."

"How'd you figure that?"

"Right after that, one of the two who'd followed him out opened the trunk."

"You saw them put the first guy in the trunk?"

"Not from where I was. All I saw was the lid pop open."

"Then how do you know they stuck him in the trunk?"

"After they closed it, they got in the car and drove away."

"How many of them did you see get in the car?"

"Two."

"And the third guy?"

She huffed. "Since I didn't see anyone lying in the driveway, I figured he was in the trunk."

"Good point," Mike said.

"Yeah."

"Yeah what?" the kid asked.

"That's a pretty good assumption."

"I thought it was, too," Mike said.

"When was this?"

"Two nights ago."

"Is that it?"

She nodded.

I sat back and tried visualizing the scene. Something just wasn't making much sense.

"You think I'm keeping something else from you?"

"I don't know yet."

"Why would I?"

"You may not know you are."

She didn't reply right off. Then she nodded. "I think I get it."

"Good. Now tell me everything you know about him."

"About who?"

"Your neighbor."

"Whaddya want to know?"

"His name. Where he lives. How you know him. That sort of thing."

She shrugged. "I think his last name's Henderson."

"You think?"

"That's what the name on his mailbox says."

"Do your parents know him?"

"Nope."

"He lives right across the street."

"So? We don't know anyone on that street."

"Really?"

"What's wrong with that?"

"It sounds so sad…"

"You're really sarcastic, you know," she said.

"It's part of my charm."

"Your what?"

"Listen…kid—"

"Tabby."

"Whatever. When I said I needed to know everything, that's what I meant."

"But why does it matter who he is or what he does?"

"Believe me, everything matters in a possible homicide."

She looked down at her lap.

"Take a guess, all right?"

"He's pretty old…almost as old as you."

"Ouch," from Mike.

Before I could get angry all over again, I reminded myself that all kids her age thought anyone over the age of twenty was old. But I said, "Kid, no one likes a smartass," just for the hell of it. "Now…describe him."

"He's pretty old, like I said. I never got very close to him, but I did see him a few times getting out of his car. I'd say he's a couple of inches taller than you, and he's got brown hair."

"What was he wearing when you saw him last?"

"A suit."

"At night?"

"He always wears a suit."

"Really?"

"Every time I see him…"

Henderson's mode of dress told me the man was a banker, broker, lawyer, undertaker, or just some weird dude who liked the way men dressed in old movies. "Is he married?"

"How should I know?"

"Ever see a woman over there?"

"I saw a blond lady there once…"

"Just once?"

"It was on a Saturday morning, but that was the only time I saw her."

"All right, I think I've got it." I grabbed my pad and began scribbling. "Around forty. Six feet tall. Brown hair. Dresses well. Probably unmarried or divorced." I looked up. "Anything else?"

"Are you gonna try and find out what happened? Or are you gonna just sit there and act like a stupid grownup who thinks all kids are assholes?"

"She raises a valid point," Mike said.

"Drop the attitude and just listen. I may very well be a stupid grownup, but I remember a lot of things I did as a kid, and not too damned many of them were very bright. But that really doesn't single me out, because whether you want to hear it or not, all kids really are stupid. But it's not your fault. It's got something to do with your frontal lobe not developing fully until you're in their mid- or late-twenties."

"So now you're holding *that* against me?"

Mike giggled. "*Touché.*"

"No," I said, "but I'm the one you came to, so cut the smartass shtick if you want me to help, okay?"

She nodded.

"Sometimes you're such a *brute*," Mike said.

"Why didn't you go to the cops about this?"

"I did. I tried calling them three different times. They kept putting me on hold."

"They're busy."

"So?"

"You should've waited."

"I'm fourteen. I don't wanna spend hours and hours on hold."

"And you tried three times?"

"The first two times they kept putting me on hold. The third time, I waited for about five minutes, and as soon as someone came on, he told me he'd get right back with me and put me on hold again, only he hung up on me…"

"That *was* kind of rude."

"See what I mean?"

"Gotcha," Mike said.

"Remember anything about the car you saw drive away?"

"It was dark."

"Anything else?"

She shook her head.

"Oh well…I guess I'll have to do what I can with what I've got."

Mike drifted over and began peeking over my shoulder.

"Think you can find out what happened?" the kid asked.

"I don't know, but I'll try." I got up and went over to the coffee station.

Her eyes grew. "What're you gonna do first?"

"Make coffee."

"Why?"

"I'm a grownup. Grownups drink a lot of coffee. I think a lot better when I'm drinking coffee. Cut out the dumb questions, okay?"

Mike drifted through the bathroom doorway when I went to rinse out the coffee pot.

"Are you gonna look into this for her?" she asked. "I really think she actually saw something bad happen."

I nodded.

"You know what else I think you should do?"

I could tell by her expression that she was about to say something I wouldn't like. "No," I whispered, "but I have a feeling I'm about to hear it anyway."

"I think you should be nicer to her."

"I *am* being nice."

"Really?"

"Don't look so surprised. Anyone else would be charging her money for this."

"But she's reporting a crime. I think that's very commendable for someone her age. She even tried reporting it to the police, and when that didn't work, she came to you."

"I know what she did. I just don't know why she came to *me*..."

"That's something you should ask her."

"I intend to."

"In the meantime, you don't have to be so *mean* about all this..."

"Whaddya mean, mean?"

"You know what I mean."

"She's got a serious attitude..."

"She's a kid. All kids have serious attitudes."

"So do I."

"I know. I'm with you almost constantly."

"Whaddya want me to do? Set her down and sing *Whistle A Happy Tune* to her?"

"Now you're being silly."

I went back out into the office, approached the coffeemaker next to my desk and dumped the water. Then I squatted, grabbed the coffee tin from the small refrigerator and dropped two scoops into the filter. I could feel the kid's eyes on me as she watched me from her chair.

"Well? What did you and your friend decide in there?"

I nearly dropped the coffee. "*What*?"

"I'm impressed," Mike said. "This cute little thing is actually pretty perceptive."

"I heard you whispering. Is that a comic relief thing, too?"

I put the can away and started up the coffee. "I mumble to myself a lot. It helps me concentrate."

"Whatever works."

"I'm glad you agree."

"Did it help?"

"Did what help?"

"Talking to yourself."

"I figured out a few things I need to do…"

"Cool. What do we do?"

"Listen…Tabitha--"

"*Tabby*…"

"Whatever. You've got to remember that this is grownup stuff, and if it's as serious as I think it might be, you need to stay out of it. I have no idea who or what we might be dealing with, so I have to be careful. If a felony were actually committed, this could get hairy--understand?"

"Then you think Mr. Henderson might be involved in something bad?"

"I have no idea. But since someone was obviously tossed in the trunk of a car in front of the man's home, I must assume that he might know or at least be involved in some way with the wrong people. I also must assume that the person tossed in the trunk could have very well been him. Understand?"

"I *think* so..."

"First thing I need to know is how you found out about me."

"One of my mom's friends at the bank knows a police detective who mentioned you. His name is Neil something. Know who I mean?"

"Your mom knows someone who knows Neil Haversack?"

She nodded.

"What else did he say?"

"She said you're a private detective."

"Anything else?"

"Nothing, really."

"Neil didn't say if I was good? Dependable? Perceptive? A solid, positive force who happens to be a credit to the profession?"

She shook her head. "He just said your rates were reasonable."

"Nice of him."

She got up. "So I guess if you don't need me anymore, you want me to go?"

"I can take it from here."

"Don't you want me to give you money or something?"

"This is actually a police matter, so I won't need any money from you. If I find out anything, I'll get with the OPD."

She looked disappointed.

"What's wrong?"

"Nothing, I guess." She went over to the door. "I'll see ya, then. Want my cell phone number? I don't know where I'll be, but you'll know how to reach me."

"Where are you going?"

"Home, I guess. I'll call ya tomorrow, if that's okay. Unless you don't want me to..."

"I think I'd better take you home."

"Huh?"

"I don't want you to--"

"It's all right. I know how to get around. I'll call ya tomorrow. Or you can lemme know what's going on..."

"I'd feel better if I drove you home."

"You worried about me or something?"

"I'd just feel better if I knew you got home okay."

"I meant it when I said I know how to get around..."

"I only care about you getting home safe and sound."

Those big baby blues watched me curiously. "Is there something you're not telling me?"

"I'm just being careful."

"How come?"

"You're just a kid. I'd feel bad if you got hit by a car on your way home."

"You really have a problem with feelings sometimes," Mike said.

"You're a strange dude, Mister Deacon," the kid said. "Cool, but strange."

"I told you she was bright," Mike said.

"Humor me, okay?"

"You old guys really are a hoot."

"Can the old guys talk, okay? Show a little respect."

"I thought I *was* showing you a little…"

"Kid, no one likes a smartass. Let me have my cup of coffee. Then I'll drive you back to your place."

She just stood there, watching me. I wondered if she was even paying attention.

"Got all that? Or weren't you listening?"

"I was listening."

"Then what's the problem?"

"You're not gonna…you know…"

"Know what?"

The blushing of her cheeks told me what was on her mind. I glanced briefly at Mike, who just shook her head.

The back of my neck bristled. "Don't even *think* about something like that, okay? I don't do stuff like that."

She was silent for a few moments. "You're not…funny, are ya?"

"Funny?"

"Funny. Gay. I've got some gay friends. They're mostly all right, but sometimes they're a tad much, especially when they get a wild hair, or when—"

34

"I'm not *gay*, dammit. And I'm sure as hell not a *pervert*."

I ignored Mike, who was trying not to laugh.

"Then what's the problem?"

"Problem?"

She looked down at her skinny chest. "I know I'm not...you know...but in a couple of years, my mom said my chest'll probably—"

"Yeah, yeah, yeah. I get all that, okay?"

"I'm just trying to—"

"Kid, you're really getting on my last nerve."

"It's *Tabby*!"

"Whatever." I went over to pour sugar in my cup.

"I'm *so* pleased the two of you are getting along so well," Mike said, smiling impishly.

35

Chapter 3

The Kendrick house, a one-story ranch painted yellow, sat in the center of the block on Fieldcrest Court in the Chateau DeVille subdivision, directly north of Oak Ridge Road.

Like its neighbors, the house had a small lot, with a palmetto bush at the corner, next to the driveway, and a row of bushes running underneath the living room window. The subdivision wasn't far from the high school, shopping, or any of the churches in the area. Judging by the appearance and condition of the houses and lots, I figured it as one of the area's older developments, most likely built when Central Florida growth was approaching its peak. As a kid, I remembered Oak Ridge Road as a relatively quiet stretch with not much on it except for a condo development or two, a couple of gas stations, and a 7-Eleven. Now, like most other areas in Central Florida, it had become an endless sea of subdivisions, condominiums, strip malls, gas stations and shopping centers, with traffic lights placed at every quarter mile.

Tabby stayed quiet on the way over. She sat beside me, her arms crossed as she gazed out the passenger window. She'd refused to put on her seat belt even though I'd insisted. It irritated me, but I couldn't blame her. The belt, made during a period of time when safety wasn't exactly fashionable, was the kind that fastened across the pelvis, making it uncomfortable and even painful if the car stopped suddenly, or hit a pothole.

Classic cars are not exactly known for comfort.

The silence was awkward but refreshing. Mike had vanished before the kid and I left the office. She'd left without a word, probably to do some spirit things she preferred not telling me about. This used to bother me in the early days of our strange relationship, but I gradually got used to it. Mike was dead but still needed her space. Since she always seemed to know instinctively when to leave me alone and when I needed her help, I saw no reason why I should do or say anything that would rock the boat.

I passed the Kendrick house and eased down the street, to the cul-de-sac.

"You just passed it." Tabby sat up.

"I don't want anyone seeing my car parked out front."

"Is this a detective thing?"

"It's a safety thing. A '75 black TransAm kind of sticks out--know what I mean?"

"Guess I didn't think of that."

"People remember classic cars. I'm pretty sure I'm the only detective in Orlando who drives one of these."

"'Kay..."

"I'm gonna turn around, drive back down to the main stretch, cut over to the next street, park there and let you walk back to your house through the back yard."

"You're not coming with me?"

"I think it would be better if no one saw me."

"Even if no one's around?"

"In this business I've learned that you can never afford to assume something like that because that's the one thing that can turn right around and bite you square on the butt." I pulled onto the main stretch, turned left, made another left onto Hearthstone, coasted halfway down the street and parked behind a beat-up tan station wagon sitting at the curb.

I could feel her staring at me as I scanned the street. "What are we doing now?"

"This is what I like to call checking out the playing field before I step up to the plate."

Her frown told me she was confused. "Is this about baseball? Or another detective thing?"

I didn't want to tell her that I wanted to make sure no one was watching her house, so I said, "It's how I work," and hoped she wouldn't ask any more questions.

She reached for the door handle. "Just don't forget to call and tell me stuff."

"I won't."

"You'll tell me as soon as you find out anything, won'tcha?"

"You'll be the first person I call."

"Really?"

"I might have to call OPD first…"

"Then I'll be the *second* person you'll call?"

"Definitely."

She opened the door. Before she got out, she turned and looked at me. Those baby blues had grown enormous again. "You sure you don't want me with ya when you start doing your detective thing?"

"I'm sure."

She jumped out and slammed the door. Then she crossed the street, went up the walk leading to someone's front yard and disappeared around the corner.

"She'll be all right." Mike had reappeared in the seat beside me.

"I hope so."

"You'll see."

I got out my cell and pressed Neil Haversack's number.

"Whaddya want, Deacon?" Neil sounded as agitated as usual. "I'm busy."

"You're also overworked, underpaid, understaffed, and just plain cranky."

"So why the hell are you calling? I don't need reminded of all that, thanks very much."

"I'm on a case right now."

"Would you like me to send the *Sentinel* an exclusive heads-up?"

"Actually, I was referred by you. And don't bother the *Sentinel* staff. I like my privacy too much."

"Someone actually had the audacity to say I *recommend* you?"

"Ironic, huh?"

"I don't know how *that* could've happened…"

"Someone was looking for a top-notch private eye in the area…"

"So why did *your* name come up?"

"Very funny."

"Get to the point, Deacon."

"I need a little help."

"I've been telling you that for years. There are two psychiatrists in this building who'd literally salivate at the prospect of having a session or two with someone like you..."

"I don't need that kind of help--not now, anyway. Maybe later."

"I take it you need some assistance with this new case? You can't handle it on your own?"

"Now what fun would that be?"

"Deacon, you realize that every time you ask for my help, I have to stick my neck out and bend a few rules that could quite possibly get my ass fired if anyone found out?"

"And I really appreciate your efforts. It makes our friendship *so* much more meaningful."

"I don't have time for this, dammit..."

"All I need is one question answered."

"I'm listening."

"This concerns a possible kidnapping and dump job that might have happened on Oak Ridge Road two nights ago."

"Got a name, by any chance?"

"It happened outside the residence of a man named Henderson."

"Henderson call it in?"

"Not exactly..."

"What exactly?"

"Henderson might be the victim."

"And you know this how?"

"An eyewitness saw it."

"That's all you got?"

"So far…"

"What's Henderson's first name?"

"Mister."

"Funny, Deacon."

"Like I said, this was reported to me by an eyewitness."

I heard him clicking his keyboard. "Nothing here…"

"The eyewitness is a girl. Fourteen years old. And you won't find it in the system."

Another click. "You're right. Why didn't she call it in?"

"She told me she tried but you guys kept putting her on hold."

"And you believed her?"

"Yeah."

"She mighta called that day we were having so much trouble with our lines. We'd been having trouble with hackers the last few weeks, and the switchboard was affected. Still, she shoulda called later on."

"She's fourteen. Fourteen-year-olds are not known for their patience."

"They're also not known to tell the truth, either, Deacon. You heard the saying: you can tell when a kid's lying the moment his lips start moving."

"I believe this one."

"Why's that?"

"She gave me too many details, for one thing."

41

"She might've seen a shitload of detective shows, for all you know. Kids usually have quite an imagination."

Sometimes Neil could be *such* an asshole…

"This could be an actual kidnapping or missing person case. So can you stop with the cynical stone-cop attitude and take this a little more seriously?"

I heard him sigh. "Go 'head…"

"All I know about this Henderson guy is that he dresses well—which tells me he's white collar. He's around forty, six feet tall, brown hair, and lives on Fieldcrest at the Château DeVille off Oak Ridge Road. The girl said she saw a man come out of his house. She also said two other men followed him outside, knocked him out and dumped him in the trunk of their car. She said this happened two nights ago."

"Any other details?"

"Like I said, I don't know much else. The girl lives across the street, but she doesn't know him either."

A pause. "And you're sure you want to take all this seriously?"

"She's a good kid. Her dad's in Iraq and her mom works at a bank on the Trail. She's not the type to make up something like this…"

"You're sure?"

"My gut's leaning that way, yeah."

"Gimme a second…"

I heard him punching keys.

About ten seconds later, the punching stopped.

Silence.

"Neil?"

More silence.

"Still there?"

"Six John Doe's have come in over the last three days. They're in the morgue right now, waiting to be identified."

"Any of them come in during the last forty-eight hours?"

"Just one."

"Any details?"

"He's badly burned up. Mostly unidentifiable. Wanna have a look anyway?"

"I think I'd better."

"I'll be here till six. Lemme know what you come up with."

"Give me a couple of hours."

I pocketed the phone.

"I heard." Mike had drifted into the front seat beside me. "This could be horrible if one of those bodies was the guy Tabby actually saw the other night."

"Right about that... But I have to find out for sure, don't I?" I fired up the ignition.

"What if one of them *is* her neighbor? What are you going to tell her?"

"I have no idea."

"She's pretty mature for her age. You might just want to tell her the truth. I think she can handle it."

"What if she can't?"

"Her father's in Iraq."

"What's that have to do with anything?"

"Going through something like that would tend to force a fourteen-year-old to mature faster than normal, wouldn't it?"

"I just don't want her to know anything until I find out for sure. Even if she is more mature than most other kids her age, something like this could freak her out. Don't forget, her mother's living there, too. If word gets out that a kidnapping and murder took place on that street, it could upset a lot of people. I think we need to keep this as quiet as possible."

"You care about her, don't you?"

I shrugged. "She's just a kid."

"So?"

"Kids have it harder nowadays. Times are rougher. There are more shitheads in government and political office than ever before, and they're screwing up everything for all of us. Besides, I can relate. I may not have had it as rough as kids nowadays but growing up sure can be a royal pain in the ass."

"You can be really sweet at times, you know."

Sometimes Mike could be downright insulting...

"I wish you hadn't said that."

"Why not? It's true."

"In this business, being sweet can get you killed."

"Still, I think you're really sweet. If I wasn't dead, I'd want to kiss you."

I couldn't believe she'd told me that. "Do you actually want to get me all turned on and

44

distracted when I'm trying to concentrate on a case? That's cruel, you know. It would be different if I could actually *do* something about it…"

"Sorry. I guess I wasn't thinking…"

It was the perfect time to change the subject. "I'm gonna drive over to the morgue and check it out. I have to determine if the burned corpse is actually her neighbor, and I think I'd better do it as quickly as possible."

"How will you know? You never saw the man, right? Neither did Tabby. You don't even have a photo."

"I can only go by my gut. And by whatever they put down as cause of death. I'm just guessing, but that's all I can do right now."

"I guess you know what you're doing."

"I should, at this stage."

"Then why do you sound doubtful?"

"There's a good reason for that."

"Because you're doubtful?"

"That's the reason."

Chapter 4

The District 9 Medical Examiner's Office sat behind some trimmed bushes on East Michigan.

About a dozen vehicles occupied the parking lot facing the long block building when I pulled in just before four o'clock. I parked two spaces down from their designated parking, next to one of their black vans. As I switched off the engine, I turned to Mike, who'd been quiet since we'd left the kid. Something was definitely on her mind. Mike wasn't usually this quiet unless something was bothering her.

"What's wrong?"

"You know why I'm here with you, right?"

"All I know is that you haven't vanished. I know that because I can see you sitting there."

"Anything else?"

"I've been wondering why you've been so quiet, but since you haven't told me anything, I can only guess. You know what kind of guy I am. If you want me to know something's wrong, you're gonna have to tell me. I'm a lousy guesser."

"Nothing's wrong, actually…"

"Then why have you been so quiet? It's not like you, you know."

"I guess I'm just trying to figure out how I can tell you that you won't be able to do this without my help."

"You mean ID'ing a guy I never actually saw before?"

"You'll definitely need my help for this."

"The kid said it was too dark to see anything, so I've got to wing it."

"Maybe not."

"You're gonna have to explain that one."

"If he's burned or unidentifiable, his spirit won't be far. I might be able to talk to him. I might even get him to tell me what happened. That's the only way we'll both know for sure."

"I hadn't thought of that."

"Anyway, that's why I'm here. I guess you realize that it won't be very enjoyable for either of us."

"Well, we did drive to the morgue. It's not exactly the perfect place for a party, or hooking up with a bunch of drunk, horny women."

"I should be able to see a wandering spirit or two while we're in there. People who die suddenly or violently stay close to their physical bodies for a while."

"Why is that?"

"When you die suddenly, you're confused and don't really know what happened. You don't even know you're dead for a while."

"Did that happen with you?"

"Yes. I know several others who've also been through the same experience."

"How long does it take to—"

"It varies. With me, it lasted a few days. With others, it takes much longer."

I could tell this was a sensitive subject. "I'll understand if you decide to split."

"I wouldn't do that to you. I just told you I'd help."

"You're spoiling me, kiddo."

She smiled. "I did that a long time ago."

We got out of the TransAm and went up the walk. I had to open the heavy glass door the conventional way, of course, while Mike just slipped through the wall and waited for me on the other side, next to the guard's desk. In other circumstances, she would have had a smirk on her face. This time, she didn't.

The place was dark and cool, and as silent as the inside of a tomb--which didn't exactly make me feel very comfortable. Although the air-conditioning had been on in the TransAm, the building was at least ten degrees cooler, and I shivered. I signed in at the desk while the guard, a big guy around forty with a shaved head and small blinking eyes, made a quick call on his radio. He told me to wait right there.

About two minutes later, a tall, slender man around thirty-five came down the hall, his shoes clicking on the polished floor. His legs were very long and thin, and his dark hair was receding in front, revealing a large, oblong forehead. He wore a white jacket and black slacks. His nametag said *WILCOX*. He slipped by me to examine the sign-in sheet and asked in a soft whisper to see my driver's license. For an instant I thought we were in a library. I handed it to him and he held it close to his face, studying it as though it was something weird swimming around in a test tube. He adjusted his thick glasses by pushing them further up his long, pointed nose with a long, pointed index finger. After about a minute he handed it back to me and straightened. Then he whispered a short, "Follow me, please."

Mike and I followed him down the long, dark corridor and slipped into the dimly lit room at the far end. He went over to the desk, picked up a clipboard and studied it. He took it with him and led us down to the other end, where the polished freezers were lined up in neat rows built into the wall. He squinted at me. "Have you been here before?"

"Once or twice."

"Detective Haversack said you're looking for someone who might've died in the last forty-eight hours?"

"Yes."

"Would you by any chance have a recent photo?"

"Sorry."

"How about a physical description?"

"I'm looking for a man about forty, six feet tall, brown hair, and always dressed in a suit."

"Anything else?"

"*Nada.*"

He stared at me for about twenty seconds before saying anything. I knew that when someone stares at you that long, when he finally says something, it won't be something you'll want to hear.

"How will you know who you're looking for?"

"I won't."

"Then why are you here?"

"I came to guess and hope I'm right. It's a game I play occasionally, whenever I'm bored, or working on a case."

He went silent again. I could tell by his scowl that he wasn't exactly thrilled by my coming here.

"I sincerely hope you're not wasting my time."

"I sincerely hope the same damned thing," I said, and gave him a friendly smile.

He didn't return my smile. He just unlocked the first freezer and pulled it out.

Mike's face turned tense and grim as she watched us.

The corpse was bloated and bruised, his features distorted and swollen. The nose and right cheekbone were broken, the face black and blue. The forehead was torn and ripped open; a large triangular flap of skin exposed the skull. What other skin was exposed had been burned to a crisp.

"What happened to him?"

"Highway accident. Apparently the gas tank exploded on impact."

I noticed the burnt shirt and workman's slacks. "He's not wearing a suit."

"It doesn't appear that he was."

"This guy didn't have much hair."

"Much of it might have been burned in the fire."

"Guess I didn't think of that one…"

He gave me one of those looks that seemed to say, *Does your mother dress you in the mornings?*

"Hair burns easily, doesn't it?"

The man began frowning at me again, making it obvious that I was taking up his valuable time. "Could this be the man you're looking for?"

"It's not him," Mike said quickly.

I glanced in her direction; she shook her head solemnly.

"No."

"Excuse me?"

"It's not him."

"You're sure?"

"Absolutely."

He pushed the drawer shut and moved on to the next. "Care to check the others?"

"I haven't had supper yet, so I guess I can take it."

The next corpse was at least fifty, bald, and bearded.

"Not him," Mike said.

The attendant glanced at me. I shook my head. He pushed the drawer shut, moved forward, and bent to open the next one.

"Who's in that one?"

"A Negro male."

Mike shook her head.

"Nope."

He straightened and approached the next one.

This drawer contained the body of a Hispanic-looking man around twenty-five, who looked to be around six feet tall and maybe a hundred and fifty pounds. His hair was thick and black, his brows thick and black, his mustache thick and black. A bullet had penetrated his short,

51

square forehead, making a hole big enough for me to bury my thumb inside. I figured a .44 mag, or possibly a .50 caliber Desert Eagle.

"Definitely not," Mike said.

I shook my head at the attendant, and he pushed the drawer shut and straightened. "These are all who've come in during the last three days. There were six, actually."

"How about the other two?"

"One is another Negro, around sixty, and the other is white, and well over eighty."

"Neither of them," Mike said.

"I think I'll pass," I told him.

He held his clipboard close to his chest. He was obviously waiting for me to leave. When I didn't move, he consulted his watch as further proof that he was busy and wanted me gone. "Is this all I can help you with?"

I glanced at Mike, who'd been watching the freezers. Judging from her expression, I guessed she might be communicating with one of the spirits. After a while, she turned to me and shook her head.

"Thanks," I told the attendant. "I think we're done here."

He led us back to the front desk. I signed out.

As we got back in the TransAm, I asked Mike, "Did you see anyone floating around in there?"

She nodded but said nothing. I could tell by her manner that she was in no mood to talk or joke around.

"Anyone talk to you?"

"They all did."

I wanted to ask more but decided not to.

"You want to ask me more, don't you?" she asked.

I nodded and started up the engine.

"Why don't you, then?"

I didn't want to get into it, so I said, "It's really not necessary, is it?"

Mike smiled. "What I said before still stands."

"What did you say before?"

"You're sweet."

"Dammit, Mike..." I put the car in reverse and backed out of the space.

Why did women have to keep being aggravating even when they were dead?

Chapter 5

Neil Haversack leaned over the desk in the lobby of the OPD building, signing someone in as Mike and I went inside.

He noticed me but didn't say anything, just gave me that same disgusted expression he always wore during working hours. He'd looked that way as long as we'd known one another. I'd think something was wrong if he actually smiled or acted pleasant. When he'd finished at the desk, he turned his back on us and without a word began walking briskly down the hall, back to his office.

"Rude," Mike said.

"That's just part of his charm," I whispered to her.

"Say something, Deacon?" Neil asked without turning.

"I just said this place has lost part of its charm. What happened? Some of the more ambitious crooks decide to pull up stakes and move to Washington, D.C. for better benefits and more job security?"

"You're quite the comedian," he said without losing a step. "You ought to try the Comedy Club and work your shtick for a *paying* audience."

"I prefer spontaneity," I said. "I don't do too well trying to remember things."

We followed him into his office, which reeked of rancid coffee left too long on the burner. I closed the door while he went right over to the coffeepot and filled a Styrofoam cup.

"What *is* that awful-smelling stuff?" Mike asked. "It smells even more horrible than the last time I came here with you."

"I don't think they've found a suitable name for it yet," I told her.

"You get used to it." Neil blew on it and turned.

"You mean your stomach actually reaches a point where it no longer feels pain?"

"Help yourself. It's free." Neil went over to his desk and dropped heavily into his chair.

Mike and I remained standing near the door. She kept staring at the pot as if it was something evil.

"If you're not gonna sit, tell me what you want so you can get outa here and I can get back to work." He glanced at his watch. "I leave for the day in half an hour."

"I made the trip to your morgue."

Neil carefully sipped the boiling liquid, frowned, and set the cup down on his blotter. He glanced behind us. "You alone?"

I glanced at Mike. "I guess you could say that's a matter of opinion..."

"I take it ya left the kid in the car."

"She's back at home. I couldn't possibly take her to the morgue."

"Why not?"

"I didn't think that would be a good idea."

Neil gave me one of his glares that clearly said, *You're an idiot.*

"A *fourteen-year-old*? In a *morgue*?"

His glare remained. "How the hell could ya make an ID, then? Or didn't ya?"

"Is he as cold and as cruel as he sounds?" Mike asked.

I winked at Mike. "None of the stiffs were a match."

"How could you tell?"

"Call it gut instinct."

Neil's glare gradually subsided and turned into mild confusion. "Like I keep saying, one of these days you're gonna have to tell me how that damned gut instinct of yours is so right on the mark."

"One of these days. What happened with that one guy? He looked like he'd been tossed in a fire and then roasted a little too long over a spit. The morgue guy said traffic accident."

"He apparently wrapped his van around a telephone pole, and the tank exploded."

"Drinking involved?"

"A trucker coming the other way swerved to avoid a twig in the road. John Doe swerved to miss the truck, and the van skidded and slammed into the pole."

"I take it the twig survived."

"Until the next guy decides not to swerve."

"This place is full of psychos who think nothing of running over defenseless twigs."

"So you came up empty, then?"

"Yeah..."

"Where you going from here?"

"I have no idea, but I really need to find out what happened as quickly as possible. There could be some dangerous people involved in this."

Neil squinted at me. "You sure the man you're looking for is actually dead?"

"No, I'm not sure. But what the little girl told me makes me think he might be."

"What makes ya think that?"

"She didn't see what actually happened because it was dark and the car obstructed her view. However, what she did see was enough to suggest that a man came out of the Henderson house and disappeared behind the vehicle parked along the curb in front of the house. Two men came out right after, moved behind the car, opened the trunk, closed it, got into the car and drove away. Unless the first guy disappeared or snuck into the car on the opposite side, I'd say it's a safe bet that he was knocked out and tossed in the trunk."

Neil thought that one over. Neil never liked making snap judgments—not even when things sounded cut and dried. Cops didn't like taking things for granted. And like all other cops I'd known, he didn't like anything that defied logic.

After a while he had another sip of the horrible-smelling coffee. "Ever consider the fact that the first guy might be *hiding* in the trunk?"

"What would be the purpose for that?"

"Suppose something's going on that isn't exactly legal, and this homeowner's involved. Say the three of them are gonna rob a place...or maybe they're going someplace where the two of them will provide a distraction while this third guy gets out of the trunk, sneaks in through the rear of this place..."

"I think I know where you're going with this."

"Well?"

"No. I didn't consider that."

"Why not?"

"It doesn't matter, does it?"

"It matters if there's no stiff."

"But something did go down, and I've got to find out what it was."

Neil nodded. "You're right. Whatever happened, a guy hiding in a trunk can't possibly be a good thing."

"And if something's going on in that neighborhood, I've got to find out. I wouldn't want that little girl or her mother to walk outside to get the mail one day and accidentally witness something that'll get either of them killed."

Neil took a deep breath and turned to his laptop. "You say the street address on the homeowner is Fieldcrest? At the Château DeVille?"

I nodded.

"And the name's Henderson?"

"You got it."

"First name? Other than Mister?"

"I honestly don't think she knows."

Neil went into his databanks. It only took him a few seconds. "Man's name is Daniel Henderson. He's forty-one and manages a hedge fund in Orlando. Worked as a broker for Morgan Stanley up until four years ago, then as a consultant at UBS, before venturing out on his own. Henderson & Associates rents office space in the Executive Center complex off Maguire Boulevard north of Colonial. It's a small operation, but they seem to be doing okay."

"Anything else?"

He clicked and checked another page. "Nothing other than a speeding ticket back in '03 and two parking tickets dated two years ago."

"Then he's clean, otherwise."

Neil gave me one of his skeptical looks. "He doesn't exactly sound like the sort that might be involved in a capital offense, like murder or kidnapping."

"That's why I've got to find out for sure."

"I think that's a really nifty idea, Deacon. Who knows? Maybe one day you'll actually turn out to be a decent private eye after all."

"You say the sweetest things, you big silly…"

"Yeah, I gotta keep a close check on that. Otherwise, the Girl Scouts'll get wind of it and camp out on my doorstep."

"Can you do us a favor while you're in such a charitable mood?"

"What's that?"

"Send a car over to her address?"

"Now why would I wanna do that?"

"I just told you something illegal might be going on over there."

"Let's just take things one step at a time, okay? You need to find out if something's going on. We still don't know if a crime was committed in the first place."

"I had a feeling you were gonna suddenly turn into a hard-ass."

Neil huffed. "Just a moment ago you called me a big silly."

"I was right on both counts, wasn't I?"

"Deacon, stop being an asshole and find out more about this before you come back and try and con me out of another favor."

"What should I do first?"

"Try doing them in order and maybe we'll start getting along better."

"I don't want to do anything that might tarnish my reputation, you know... Clients don't like detectives who follow the rules. Clients like misfits and badasses. I guess that's why I make the big bucks."

"I mean it, Mr. Misfit. You really need to get on top of this one. And don't worry about that kid. Trust me--kids are different these days. Today's fourteen-year-old has more savvy and street sense than a twenty-year-old in our day."

"I'll keep my eyes and ears open. And I'll be careful."

"You'd better be."

"You're worried. But I'll keep it our little secret. I wouldn't want anyone in this building to know that deep-down, you're really just a big sack of mush."

"Keep it up. One of these days you'll catch me when I'm in a sour mood."

"Tell those Girl Scouts I said hi." I opened the door.

"Just don't get yourself shot."

"You know, you really *are* just one large sack of mush."

"I just don't like paperwork, asshole."

I closed the door behind me and turned to Mike. "See there? He's not nearly as bad as you think."

Mike just shook her head.

***

Once I left the OPD building, I stopped at Domino's Pizza, ordered a small pepperoni & sausage pizza, and was on my way back to Oak Ridge Road by seven o'clock.

The rush hour was just about over. Bumper-to-bumper traffic had tapered down to static groups, causing the usual congestion at the lights and intersections. It was just before seven-thirty when I reached the shopping plaza down the road from the Château DeVille to eat my pizza.

I parked near the end aisle in the huge lot, about a hundred feet from the Goodwill Store, the front of the TransAm facing the main highway. People flocked to the supermarket and the buffet restaurant next to it, pushing their carts and leaving them in the middle of the aisles when they'd finished unloading their purchases. A tall, slender woman about forty years old cleaned out her cart and pushed it over to the cart pen, leaving it about two feet short, directly behind someone's white BMW. I wanted to tell her she was a lazy bitch but knew how that would end up. She'd tell me to mind my own business or panic and grab her cell to call 911 and tell them she was being attacked, and I'd have to shoot her or have sex with her just to shut her up. I decided I didn't need the aggravation—especially when I was enjoying my pizza. I watched her drive away in her glistening white Charger and focused on the passing traffic roaring down Oak Ridge.

Mike had disappeared about an hour ago. I hadn't heard a word from her since, so I was on my own once again. I didn't have a definite plan in the works and knew my best bet was to improvise and hope for the best. It was too late in the day to visit Henderson's office, so I decided to check things out at his home. Once I'd finished eating my pizza, I'd drive over to the Château DeVille and park somewhere on Hearthstone where I could monitor Henderson's house. Since his place was right across the street from where the kid and her mother lived, I had to be extremely cautious. This in itself wouldn't be difficult for me. I'd been in this business a long time and was pretty damned good at being cautious.

However, I had no idea what I should be looking for. Blood stains at the curb? In the street? On the walk? Signs of a scuffle? I didn't know. I only knew that if the kid had been right about what she'd seen, a crime had been committed, and I had to find out what happened.

I just hoped that the people involved would never find out that the little girl across the street had called the police to report something she'd seen happening in front of the house and then had gone to a private detective to make sure someone began looking into it.

Chapter 6

At around 8:00, I finished my pizza, got back onto Oak Ridge, and turned right at the Château DeVille entrance.

I passed Fieldcrest, made the left onto Hearthstone, and found a place to park. Since more than half a dozen other vehicles sat at the curb, I could remain inconspicuous. It was dark, and no one was about. I stuck my .380 Cheetah automatic in the side pocket of my windbreaker, grabbed my penlight and lock-pick case from my glove box, and got out of the TransAm.

Since I had only a hundred yards or so to walk, I took my time and went down the street that passed the kid's backyard. I could use the bushes lining the Kendrick property to cross the street and then hide in the bushes surrounding Henderson's house while I scanned the surroundings. The streetlamps at the end of the street and halfway down to the cul-de-sac provided sufficient haze to make me less invisible, so I knew I had to be extra careful.

I crept up to the front of the Kendrick house and listened. I heard only the usual muffled sounds coming from a television set. I crossed the street and made my way straight for the rose bush that had taken over the corner of Henderson's house, concealing a fairly large portion of the building. Once I'd squeezed behind it, I squatted down and stayed there a couple of minutes, listening. I pressed my ear to the warm brick wall but heard nothing. The hazy, rectangular-shaped glare lighting up a portion of the front yard was obviously the living room light reflecting onto the lawn. I had to assume someone was home—which meant I couldn't sneak into the house. I also couldn't cross the front yard without the risk of being noticed. Unless I had a good story ready, my best bet was to get back to the TransAm and figure out my strategy when I visited Henderson's offices the next morning.

I was about to get up from my position in the bushes when I heard Mike's voice a few feet away, on my right.

"Stay there and don't move."

I immediately froze.

In the next few seconds, I heard approaching footsteps in the grass. Someone had obviously seen me or suspected someone was in the yard. My pulse hammered, but I didn't move. I wanted to reach for the .380 but didn't want to risk making any noise.

The shifting of footsteps continued, growing louder. I figured that in about thirty seconds, whoever was out there would be just a few feet away.

Just then, the buzzing of a cell phone broke the silence about twenty feet away. The shifting stopped suddenly. Then I heard a gasp, a frenzied "Shit!" and the footsteps began moving away quickly.

"Now you can get out of here," Mike said.

I straightened, squeezed out from behind the rosebush and trotted across the front yard, toward the street. I was just a few feet from the sidewalk when I heard a door open behind me.

"Don't turn around," Mike said behind me.

Once again, I did as she said. I crossed the street, went down the walk a few yards, veered off into the grass and walked up the drive of the house next to the Kendrick house. I climbed the front steps, but instead of approaching the door, I cut to the right, darted through the yard, came back out and crossed the street, making my way back to Hearthstone, where the TransAm awaited me.

**

Mike appeared in the seat beside me as I got in behind the wheel.

"What the hell happened back there?" My pulse was still racing. "Was someone checking out the yard?"

"I got there and saw someone coming out through the back. He was being really quiet, so I was suspicious. Also, he had a gun, and that made me even more suspicious."

"You saw a gun?"

She nodded.

"Someone was actually walking around the house back there carrying a *gun*? In a *subdivision*?" The full impact of the situation surprised me. It also told me something highly illegal and possibly criminal was going on in that house.

"It was definitely a gun."

"Is there more to this?"

66

"I watched him for a little while to see what he was doing, and when I saw him standing near the bushes, staring at the rosebush, he took a gun out of his pocket and fitted it with a silencer. That told me he was up to no good and would probably shoot you."

"A *silencer*?"

"Yes."

"This is beginning to look like Henderson got himself involved with some really bad people."

"Looks like it."

"If there's mob activity operating in that neighborhood, things'll get ugly really fast." I started up the ignition and pulled away from the curb. "Did you by any chance find out who's staying inside the house?"

"Not really. I got there just as the guy came out through the back."

"Did you get a good look at him?"

"Who? The guy with the gun? Or the guy at the front door?"

"Either."

"Well, the guy with the gun looked Hispanic."

"How about the other guy?"

"He looked Hispanic, too."

I pulled out onto the main stretch and headed west. I thought about what happened and found myself wondering again. "What was the deal with the cell phone?"

"I didn't want him to shoot you."

"You mean—"

"I made it go off to distract him."

"Well, it certainly did that. It sounded like it pissed him off, too."

"I didn't care if I pissed him off. I just wanted him to turn around and walk away."

"I believe you saved my life once again, my dear."

"It worked, didn't it?"

I stopped at the red light and tried to absorb all this. "If Henderson wasn't there, what were those two doing in his house? What sort of guy who runs his own hedge fund business lets two Hispanics stay at his house—especially when one of them is walking around the property with a gun and silencer?"

"Someone who had no choice?"

"But why the gun?"

"They didn't want anyone snooping around."

"Why not?"

"You wouldn't want anyone snooping around *your* place, would you?"

"I wouldn't exactly step outside with a gun and shoot whoever I found out there."

"Makes me wonder if he actually would have shot you."

"I'm glad he didn't get the chance."

"Do you really think the Mob's involved in this?"

"I'm more concerned about what those two are protecting."

***

That night, the kid called me a little after eleven o'clock, as I was sitting in the living room in front of the TV, slowly downing a glass of Jack.

On the screen, Bogie was having an uncomfortable conversation about brain surgery with Sidney Greenstreet on Turner Classic Movies. Mike had left before I got home; I didn't think I'd see her for a while.

"Did you find out anything?" she asked.

"Who *is* this?" I had to know for sure.

"It's Tabby. Can't you recognize my voice?"

I was surprised and a little irritated by her call. When I was her age, I wasn't allowed to call anyone at such a late hour. Then I figured that since she was using her cell phone, her mother probably thought her daughter was asleep, and had no idea she was calling anyone. When I was the kid's age, cell phones hadn't been invented yet.

"Why are you up so late?"

"School's been out for a week."

"It's still late."

"So…did you find out anything?"

Apparently the kid wasn't in the mood to discuss the lateness of the hour with me. Lucky for her I was slightly mellow from the Jack and not as concerned about her attitude as I might have been if I'd been sober. "I'm sure glad we got that cleared up. And to answer your question, maybe. Now go to bed." I had another sip of my drink. I usually kept tight-lipped during a working case for several reasons. In this case, I didn't think it would be wise to tell a fourteen-year-old that two strange men were staying in the house across the street from her, and at least one of them was armed with a gun and didn't like trespassers.

"Whaddya mean?"

"I mean go to bed."

"What's "maybe" mean?"

"Last I checked the old Thorndike-Barnhart, "maybe" meant "perhaps." It could also mean "yes." But then again, it could also mean "no." In some cases, it might even mean "neither.""

She groaned. "You know what I mean, so quit being a butthole."

"I'd rather not say right now. And watch your language. And while you're doing that, show a little respect."

"Are you drinking?"

"Why do you ask?"

"You sound…funny."

"I *am* funny. Now go to bed."

"Why can't you tell me what's going on?"

"I don't like discussing a case until I've figured out what I'm dealing with and what's involved."

"But you just said—"

"I said maybe—which means I *might* have found out something."

"Then why won't you tell me?"

"It could also mean that I didn't actually find out anything."

"Which is it?"

"I'm not sure…"

"Deacon, are you playing with me?"

"It's too damned late for me to be playing with anyone."

"That doesn't answer my question."

"Not exactly."

"What *are* you doing, then?"

"I'm trying to keep you in the dark."

"How come?"

"As I told you before, I don't want you getting involved in this."

"Then you *did* find out something."

"I'm not at liberty to say."

She went silent.

"I'm really doing you a favor, you know. If something bad *is* happening, you're better off not knowing anything."

"So you think—"

"I don't know *what* I think—not yet, anyway."

"When *will* you know?"

"Tomorrow, maybe."

"Seriously?"

"Or the day after. It depends."

"On what?"

"A lot of things."

"Such as…?"

"If people talk to me. If I find out anything worthwhile. If I come up with a valuable clue. If I hear of something going down."

I heard her sigh. "When will I know?"

"When I call and tell you."

A pause. "I guess I should just shut up and let you do your job…"

"Spoken like a trooper."

"Huh?"

"That means yeah, you nailed it."

"All right, then. I'll wait till you call me again."

"See ya later. And kid?"

"Tabby."

"Whatever. Do me a favor."

"What is it?"

"Don't go over there."

"Where?"

"Where do you think? The Henderson house."

"I won't."

"Promise?"

"Uh-huh…"

"Say it."

"Say what?"

"Say you promise."

Another sigh, this one deeper. "I promise I won't go over there. Satisfied?"

"I guess that'll have to do for now. Talk to you later."

I hung up, finished my drink and poured another. Then I watched Bogie dumping his wife in the mountains so he could spend the rest of his life happily ever after with her kid sister Evelyn, played by a young Alexis Smith.

When I could no longer keep my eyes open, I shuffled straight off to bed.

DAY TWO

Chapter 7

The next morning, I got up at eight, showered and fixed breakfast. Once I'd finished with the dishes, I took two aspirin for my slight hangover and was on the road by nine.

Henderson & Associates, as Neil had told me, kept their offices in Executive Center on Maguire Boulevard. That complex of office buildings sat in a well-maintained circle just half a mile north of Colonial Drive. The long brick buildings all consisted of just two or three floors and sat behind professionally trimmed bushes on a professionally-mowed lawn.

The parking lot behind the building was nearly filled. I found a vacant spot near the end and parked.

"This is nice." Mike materialized beside me and began looking around. "Is this where that man Henderson runs his office?"

"Yes."

She smiled. "It's very pretty, actually. Those flowers growing next to the side entrance are beautiful. Someone obviously waters them every day."

"Very aesthetic," I commented. "Are you hinting that I should pick you a bouquet?"

"Now what would I want with a bouquet of flowers?"

"You definitely raise a valid point."

"Thank you." She glared.

I knew right then that I should cut out the smartass quips or she'd disappear, and I needed her right now.

"So now that I'm here, what do you want me to do?"

"Hopefully, nothing. If things don't go south, I should only need you for backup."

"What are you gonna do?"

"I hope I can just walk in and talk with Henderson. I might be able to pick up some vibes—or at least find out what's going on in his house."

"And if they don't let you see him?"

"Then you slip into his office and find out why he doesn't want to see me."

"What if he's not in?"

"Take a look at his desk and see what you can find."

"You mean like messages? Notes? Things like that? I can't open a filing cabinet or safe. I hope you know that."

"Can't you look *inside* a safe?"

"Depends."

"On what?"

"If I really want to…"

It was beginning to become quite clear that Mike was in one of her moods. I decided not to make this situation any worse.

"Just play it by ear, okay? I'll take whatever you can give me."

We got out, went up the steps and entered the building. The a/c kept the lobby at least ten degrees cooler than outside. The directory listed Henderson & Associates as being on the second floor, and as we waited, a short, slender blonde in a snug business suit walked over and stopped a few feet in front of me, checking the folder she held in front of her. She smelled strongly of lavender and her hair looked like it had been professionally done by someone expensive. I wanted to stare at her in the worst way, but since Mike was standing beside me, I forced myself to behave. It was disrespectful to ogle a woman while you were with another woman. I figured the rules would be different if the woman you were with was dead, but Mike's expression strongly suggested I should honor the unspoken code.

As soon as the elevator door slid open, Mike and I followed the girl into the cool, carpeted car. She pressed the button for the second floor, then turned and asked in a tiny, high-pitched voice which floor I'd like.

"You just pressed the right button," I said, smiling.

If she'd caught the innuendo, she didn't let on. She just smiled briefly and turned back around.

"That was *so* tacky," Mike said flatly.

I nodded and felt even guiltier.

I spent the ten-second trip trying not to stare at the girl's ass, but it was difficult with Mike watching me. The loud *ding*! signaling the end of our trip snapped me back to reality, and I had to look as if I was ignoring the girl as she trotted down the hall.

But at least she went in the same direction I was headed, and just before she opened the door, I caught the delicious sight of her bending over to pick up a piece of paper that had slipped out of her folder.

I followed her in and closed the door behind us. When I turned, I saw that Mike had already disappeared.

"Help you?"

The receptionist was extremely large, with a distinct Jabba-the-Hut presence, huge breasts, and a loose, jowly face. Her cold gaze just above her thick-rimmed glasses made my testicles feel unnaturally exposed, and I subconsciously turned sideways just in case a random batch of radiation had escaped her. I know it sounds weird, but I felt sincerely sorry for her chair.

"I'd like to talk to Mr. Henderson."

Her thick black brows mashed together, forming a square-shaped wedge of flesh bulging between them. "Are you a client?"

"No..."

The brows remained mashed together. "Then please state your business."

"It's personal."

"Which firm do you represent?"

I hadn't counted on this. "I'm independent."

"Name?"

"Crossman." It was the first name that popped into my head. It was the brand name of my first pellet rifle. I didn't know why I was thinking of firearms at the time. Perhaps it was because this woman was pressing all the wrong buttons and I wanted to kill her the slowest way possible.

"Have you talked with Mr. Henderson before?"

"No."

"Will this be a matter of investment?"

"Yes..."

"Will you be able to give this firm three different business references?"

I groaned and fought down the urge to whip out my .380 instead. The pellet gun just wouldn't cut it anymore. "Yes. Probably. Maybe. Perhaps."

Apparently she didn't like my answers. The lump of flesh between her brows grew even larger. "Which *is* it?"

"Pick one."

She lowered her gaze and began attacking her keyboard. I was just about to turn around when she stopped clicking. I expected her to tell me to have a seat. Instead, she said, "Mr. Henderson can't see you today."

"Why not?"

"He hasn't been in his office the last three days."

I thought of my .380 again. "When do you expect him in?"

"He hasn't called to say when he'll be coming in."

"And you don't know where he is?"

"No."

"But you knew he wasn't in the office already."

"Yes."

Now I wanted to forget the .380 altogether and see if I could possibly staple her tongue to her nose before anyone else noticed. "And you managed to grill me over the coals for the last five minutes anyway."

"Sir, I am required to ask all of our visitors—"

"I understand."

She went back to her keyboard. "I can arrange for you to see one of Mr. Henderson's colleagues."

"Now why would I want to see one of his colleagues?"

She looked up and stared. The wad of flesh between her brows began to quiver. I'd probably confused her.

"Sir, what exactly is the nature of this visit?"

"I wanted to see Henderson. I didn't want to see anyone else, and I'm pretty sure that means I don't want to see one of his colleagues."

"But as I just told you—"

"I know. He's not in."

"If he was in, I'd—"

"I know, but he's not, so you can't, can you?"

She stared at me the longest time. Then shook her head.

"Then I guess I can't see him, can I?"

"You can't if he's not in."

"Thanks. I'm glad we finally cleared that up."

***

Mike was waiting for me out in the hall.

"I take it they didn't tell you anything," she said.

"Actually, they told me less than nothing."

"How is that possible?"

"I don't know, but they somehow managed."

We left the building.

"I'm glad I went in there and looked around," Mike said as we got back in the TransAm.

"Find anything interesting?"

"There were two photos on Henderson's desk. Both were of the same man, but with two different women. The man I saw standing at the front door last night definitely wasn't the man in the photos."

"You're sure?"

"Positive."

"Describe the man in the photos."

"He fits Tabby's description. Fairly tall, brown hair, and well-dressed..."

"And the man at the house?"

"Just as I told you last night—he looked Hispanic."

"Interesting."

"Are you thinking the same thing I'm thinking?" she asked.

"Are you thinking of having a bacon cheeseburger and fries for lunch?"

"Of course not."

"Then I'll say no."

"Be serious, now..."

"Could you be thinking that maybe the kid's been right about this all along? That a crime

79

actually did occur across the street from her place?"

"Exactly."

I pulled out my cell, punched Neil's number, and waited for my Bluetooth to complete the call.

"I'm busy, Deacon." His voice barked loudly from the tiny speaker in the unit clipped to my visor.

"He's *so* rude..." Mike shook her head.

"Neil, I think something's definitely going on. Henderson hasn't been in his office in three days."

"Are his people worried about it?"

"They don't seem to be."

"He runs the company, doesn't he?"

"I guess so. The company bears his name, anyway..."

"Maybe he's out of town."

"They didn't say he was."

"Maybe they didn't think you were important enough to be told his private itinerary."

"That's cold, Neil..."

"Or maybe they just don't like giving out personal information to just anyone who comes in off the street."

"Maybe..."

"If something unexpected came up, they wouldn't want to tell anyone about it—especially someone they don't know. For all they knew, you could have been a competitor."

"Possibly."

"Why just possibly?"

80

"This whole thing is beginning to stink, big-time. I went to Henderson's house last night. Two men were staying there, and neither was Henderson."

"What the hell were ya doing there in the first place?"

"Snooping around. It's my job, remember?"

"Deacon...if I have to haul your ass in for criminal trespass—"

"You won't."

"Tell me exactly what you did."

"I went over there to see if I could find anything. What I found was someone sneaking around in the back."

"How do you know he was sneaking around?"

"He had a gun. And he also had a silencer. I could tell he didn't have it just as a conversation piece, or to look dangerous."

"What happened?"

"I managed to get out of there. Otherwise, I'd be dead, and we wouldn't be having this pleasant conversation."

A pause. "I know better than ask how you managed to get out of that predicament, but you'd better tell me how you know Henderson wasn't there."

"There was another man there who wasn't Henderson. I saw him at the front door while I was sneaking away."

"And you're sure he wasn't Henderson?"

"Positive."

Silence.

"Still there?"

"Deacon, you know there could be a slew of possible scenarios here. Henderson could have relatives staying there. Or friends. Or business associates. He could've rented out his house, for all you know. Since his own company doesn't seem too broken up over the fact that he hasn't been in his office--"

"I have this strong feeling something happened to him."

"You could be right. You could also be very wrong. If you are, you could be getting yourself in serious legal trouble."

"I still have to find out if something bad or illegal is going on. Don't forget--a fourteen-year-old and her mother live across the street."

"I hear ya."

"Mature or not, she's fourteen. Maybe I'm a little old-fashioned, but I'd really like to see her reach fifteen. And if something's going on in that house, she might find herself in the wrong place one day and accidentally get shot, or worse."

"Know where you're going from there?"

"I've got an idea or two." I knew better than tell Neil I had no clue. Whenever I told him something like that, he usually made some crude remark that made me consider going into another line of work. After all, I was a dynamite private eye and had to live up to my reputation. I always had to have some idea of what I was going to do. Otherwise, it made me look like an idiot. Or worse—an amateur. "I'll let you know what I find out."

"You've got my number." He hung up.

"What's your idea?" Mike asked as we stopped at the intersection at Curry Ford and Semoran.

"Actually, I don't have one."

"Then why'd you tell your surly friend—"

"I don't want him to think I'm a dumbass. And he's not surly, he's just overworked, underpaid, and constipated."

"Well, that horrible coffee he drinks all day can't possibly be good for *anyone*."

"He's used to it. Actually, he'd probably be even harder to deal with if he didn't drink it."

Mike was silent for a few moments. "You must have *some* idea what you're gonna do…"

"Maybe, maybe not."

"Tell me the maybe part."

"It'll definitely require your assistance again."

"I figured as much."

"I'll make this simple. I've got to find out who's actually staying in that house."

"In other words, you want me to go over there and pay them a visit?"

"That sounds like a terrific idea. I wish I'd thought of it."

"Something tells me you already did."

The light changed; we started moving again.

"So what do you want me to do once I go on in and start looking around?"

"Find out what you can and get back to me. I'll be parked along the curb down the next street, as before."

"That sounds simple."

"Something tells me that if the man you saw at the front door isn't Henderson, he's probably just as dangerous as his buddy. Anyone who posts an armed man outside a house in a subdivision has got to be dangerous—or crazy. Or both."

"You don't think your cop friend is right?"

"Why would a relative or renter have someone sneaking around the place with a gun?"

"Good point. It makes me wonder what they're actually hiding in there."

"That's what we've got to find out."

"And then we've got to find out what the two of them are doing there, right?"

"Unfortunately, that's not going to be the hardest part of all this."

"What *is* the hardest part?"

"Finding out what actually happened to Henderson…"

Chapter 8

We reached the Château DeVille just before twelve o'clock.

The lunch hour traffic was horrible, but the development was relatively quiet. I checked out Fieldcrest by making a leisurely drive down the street, turning around at the cul-de-sac and heading back down to the other end. There were no cars parked in front of the Henderson house and no activity in the living room window or anywhere on the property.

"Doesn't look like much going on," Mike said as we passed the house.

"That doesn't mean the house is empty."

"I'll find out for sure."

"While you're in there, I'm going over to the supermarket to get some lunch. I'll try to make it quick, but I can't guarantee anything in all this traffic."

"I'll find you." Then she vanished.

The shopping plaza traffic was so hectic that I had to park at least twenty spaces down from the supermarket. Judging by Mike's work in the past, I figured she wouldn't take much more than fifteen minutes before she found out something and came back. Mike was amazingly quick when it came to finding things out. But it only stood to reason. When you could slip through walls and listen to people talk without them seeing you, you didn't have to worry about complications.

I selected a chili dog and potato salad at their deli and grabbed a small bottle of Sierra Mist on my way to checkout. I paid and went back out. As I approached the TransAm, I noticed a shopping cart sitting in front of my door, its corner less than two inches from the metal. I looked around quickly but didn't see any obvious sign of a guilty party. I pulled it carefully out of the way, silently wished the perpetrator a long, lingering illness followed by a slow, painful death, then got in the car and began eating my lunch.

Mike came back just as I was finishing the last scoop of potato salad. She didn't look pleased. "This case is getting worse and worse."

"I take it you found out something?"

"They obviously did something to Henderson. There are three of them—two men and a woman. The woman wasn't there, but I've got this feeling she's a stripper."

"How do you know?"

"Her name is Heather. And both of them mentioned her dance routine at the club."

"That would make it a fairly good clue. What else is going on?"

"The guy I saw at the front door last night—his name is Paco."

"What about the other guy?"

"They called him Sanchez."

"Did you find out what they're doing there?"

"They were waiting for something."

"Some*thing*? Or some*one*?"

"Both, actually. Paco was on the phone, and whoever he was talking to was asking him directions."

"And they didn't mention Henderson?"

"All the other guy said was that everything was set up and they were done with him."

"Set up?"

"That's what I heard."

"Anything else about this stripper?"

"I have this strong feeling she might be in charge of all this."

"How'd you get that?"

"Paco called her at least three times while I was there. He asked her all sorts of questions about Henderson and also about times and dates. He didn't order her to do anything and he wasn't condescending or anything like that. In fact, he seemed almost respectful of her."

"Respectful?"

"That's how he sounded—to me, anyway."

"That still doesn't tell us what's going on. The only thing that tells me an actual crime was committed was what was said about their being done with Henderson. This is beginning to sound like some sort of kidnapping--or maybe even an extortion scheme."

"But we don't know anything else."

"Did Paco or Sanchez mention anything about last night?"

"Paco did say something about keeping an eye out. He said he didn't like anyone wandering around, like last night, when he saw someone cutting through the yard."

"Sanchez didn't mention his cell going off?"

"Not that I heard…"

"Did you hear anything about the time or day of whatever they're waiting for?"

"No, but I have a feeling it'll be soon."

"Then I've got to drive back over there and wait."

"For what?"

"For someone else to show up."

***

Surveillance is an important part of a private eye's job.

It's also the bane of the profession, and a major reason why many detectives quit the business. Sitting in a car for hours at a time can literally be a pain in the ass, as well as hell on the bladder. If you don't mind peeing in a cup or entertaining yourself with endless games on your iPad, you'll eventually go bonkers. That's why it helps to have a partner—or dead buddy—with you to break the monotony.

Mike and I waited in the TransAm from 12:30 to well past two. Since I'd parked on Hearthstone, the front entrance of Henderson's place was in clear view from my passenger window. The windows of the TransAm were heavily-tinted, of course—a necessity in Central Florida. The tint made me much less visible from the outside, but by the same token, it was much more difficult to see through the binoculars. But I had no choice. In a subdivision, using binoculars to watch a house can turn ugly. I just hoped no one would come out of their house, rap on my window, and ask why I was parked on their street.

At two-thirty, I asked Mike to go back to the house and stay there. I needed to drive back to the supermarket and relieve myself in the john. The Sierra Mist had been working on me, and since I didn't have an empty cup available, I didn't want to spend the next couple of hours sitting in the car, trying to concentrate with a full bladder.

Fifteen minutes later, I came back and parked on the same side of the street, about two car lengths back. From this vantage point, I could see the front of Henderson's house as well as the back of the Kendrick house. Mike hadn't returned, but that didn't concern me. Knowing her as well as I did, I figured she'd heard or seen something and decided to stay there to find out what was going on.

She came back a few minutes later, materializing just as I was wiping off the lens of the binoculars with a Kleenex.

"Anything interesting going on over there?"

"They're definitely expecting a visitor. Paco's sitting by the living room window with his cell in his hand. He's been talking to a woman for the last twenty minutes."

"The stripper?"

"It sounded like the same voice on the line. They're talking about the guy who's bringing over a package."

"What sort of package?"

"They didn't say. The woman sounded nervous, but Paco kept saying this guy was dependable, and that she shouldn't worry."

"Why was she so nervous?"

"She kept mentioning the big man, and that they had to be really careful so he couldn't find out, because if he did, they'd all be dead."

"Did they happen to let a name slip out?"

"No."

"What about Sanchez? What was he doing during all this?"

"He was watching the property."

"I haven't seen him."

"He's out in the Florida room, cleaning his gun. You can't see that part of the house from here, but he was definitely watching the backyard. Every couple of minutes he'd come back in, walk straight into the dining room and stand in front of the window for a few minutes."

"He's obviously still nervous about last night."

"He did seem nervous."

"He's the one who scares me the most."

"Because he's got a gun?"

"A lot of guys have guns, and a lot of them carry guns. Sanchez scares me because he's so attached to his. You don't see me walking around with my piece or cleaning it all the time, do you?"

"Are you saying you've got a dirty gun?"

"You should only have to clean a gun after you use it. Nowadays you really don't have to clean a gun very much at all. They make cleaner loads for both automatics and revolvers than they did years ago. When you go through a lot of ammo, you'll have to clean the gun more often because excessive cordite from the explosions will pit the barrel and build up a residue that will eventually cause a gun to explode in your face. A man who spends so much of his time cleaning his gun is definitely someone who uses it too much. This makes me nervous."

"I see."

I picked up the binoculars and had another look. It only took me a second to see something that made me cringe in my seat.

"Dammit!"

"What's wrong?"

I groaned. "It's the kid..."

"What's she doing?"

"The worst thing ever. She's walking over to the damned house!"

***

Mike immediately vanished. She'd probably gone over there to distract Sanchez.

I had to get over there, too—and fast. I couldn't let Sanchez or Paco get their hands on the kid. It was bad enough that they'd probably be able to see the kid's face—especially if she got any closer. If they were as bad as Mike and I suspected, this wouldn't be good for the kid *or* her mother.

Then it dawned on me: I *couldn't* go over there. If I did, it would tell them they were under observation--which would destroy the case entirely. It would probably get both the kid and her mother killed.

But I had to do *some*thing…

I grabbed my cell, found her number on my call list and pressed it. My pulse hammered as I waited. Hopefully, the kid had her cell with her. Hopefully, she'd hear it and might even answer it. Hopefully, she'd listen to me this time and realize that she'd made a big mistake. Maybe she'd even do as I said this time.

I realized right off that I was being overly optimistic. She might be mature for her age, but she was still a kid and most likely wouldn't listen to anything I said. When you're a kid, anyone over the age of twenty is the enemy, and not to be trusted. She obviously felt this same way because she wouldn't have done what she was doing right now if she'd trusted me in the first place.

My skin crawled. Why the hell was she going over there? Whatever did she think she could accomplish? I'd told her something bad might be happening over there, so why the hell would she even consider doing such a stupid—

"Hi…" She'd obviously picked up on my call.

"What the hell are you doing?"

"Doing?"

"Yeah. Doing—as in *not* doing."

"Whaddya talking about? I'm in my room, just like you told me…"

"The hell you are. You're in the middle of the street, and you're about to be in very serious trouble if you don't turn around right this second and go back home. And stay put this time!"

"How'd ya know?" I took a gander through my binoculars. She was looking around.

"Just do as I say, dammit!"

"Are you...*watching* me from somewhere?"

"No, I'm using my special ESP talents. Of *course* I'm watching you. Now turn right around and go back to your house!"

"I don't think she should do that." Mike had returned. She sat next to me, her eyes bigger than I'd seen them in a long time.

"What's wrong?"

"Sanchez just came out of the house, through the back. He was looking right at her when he came out."

It came to me in a flash. "My God... If he sees her go back to her house..."

"Deacon?" It was the kid. "Who're you talking to?"

"My guardian angel. Listen to me. Whatever you do, don't go back to your house."

"Why not?"

"Do you happen to see that guy coming around from the back of the house?"

"Uh-huh..."

"You don't want him to know where you live."

"Why not?"

"Just do as I say and stop asking stupid questions. Turn right around, hurry down the street, go past three or four houses and slip through someone's yard. I'll meet you on Oak Ridge. Do it now!"

No reply.

"Be back in a minute." Mike vanished again.

I held up the binoculars just in time to see Sanchez approaching the kid.

"*Dammit…*" I dropped the binoculars, started up the engine, and pulled out of the spot. I was just about to cross the main highway when Mike came back. "Go pick her up."

"What did you do?"

"I made his cell phone go off just when he was about to talk to her. As soon as he took it out and tried to figure out why no one was on the line, Tabby slipped away. I think maybe she did figure out what you were trying to tell her."

"Wonders never cease." I pulled out and cruised down the street. I was about to turn right on Oak Ridge when I saw her emerging from someone's backyard two houses down.

Chapter 9

The kid opened the passenger door, climbed in, and slammed it shut.

I peeled away, quickly blending into a small gap between two clots of passing traffic. We cruised down Oak Ridge for about a block. When I felt we were a safe distance away, I made a quick right and pulled into the gas station at the corner.

"That was really cool!" Twisted around in the seat, she was watching the back as I pulled beside a pump and waited for my heart rate to slow down.

"*Cool*? You thought that was *cool*?" I could barely contain myself. This kid could have gotten herself killed. She'd also nearly screwed up this entire case. Now she was acting as if she'd just gotten off the roller coaster at a theme park.

"She's just a kid." Mike appeared directly behind me in the back seat. "I know she messed up, but that's all over now. Just take a deep breath and think about what we have to do."

I took a deep breath, but that just didn't cut it. Deep breaths were okay when you were just issued a speeding ticket. They were also fairly tolerable when you were just told by the babe with you that she didn't want to have sex even though you'd just spent a hundred bucks on her dinner and drinks.

This was *much* worse. This involved two strange Latinos who might be Mob-connected and may have murdered the kid's neighbor. One of them carried a gun and nearly used it on me the night before. I didn't want to imagine what would have happened if Sanchez had coaxed the kid into the house.

"It didn't work," I told her. "I'm still pissed."

"What didn't work?" The kid was looking at me.

"Take another breath," Mike said.

I took another one and shook my head. "Nope. I'm still pretty hot."

"Who're you talking to?" The kid was glancing at the back seat, where Mike sat.

"Myself," I said.

"Again?"

I shrugged. "No one else seems to want to listen to me. You don't, do you? If you did, you wouldn't have just committed the world's worst boner by going over there."

She moved closer to the door and didn't say a word. She knew I was hot. She probably also knew that she'd make the situation even worse if she said anything.

"You could've gotten yourself in serious trouble back there," I told her.

"But all I did was—"

"You have no idea who those people are, do you?"

"Who are they?"

"That's not exactly the issue."

"Do *you* know who they are?"

"Not exactly…"

She shrugged a shoulder. "Then why are you so freaked?"

"Kid, you really need to stop asking questions and start listening to what I'm trying to tell you."

"How many are there? I never saw that one guy before…"

"You didn't even hear me, did you?"

"I heard you. I just wanna know what's going on…"

"You're much better off if you just stop being curious and let me handle this myself."

"All I did was walk over there. I was gonna ask them about Mr. Henderson. What's so stupid about that?"

"Listen to me…and try to understand. The people in that house don't want *anyone* talking to them or even seeing them."

"But who *are* they? And what happened to Mr. Henderson?"

"That's what I'm trying to find out. Isn't that why you came to me in the first place?"

"Something…happened to him, didn't it?"

"I'm not sure. I think so."

"But…who *are* those dudes? And why are they staying there?"

"I haven't figured that out yet."

She shrugged. "Maybe they're just relatives… I told you, we only know a couple of people on that block. They could be friends of his, couldn't they?"

"I don't think so, but since you've already put yourself in the middle of all this, I've got to tell you that I'm pretty sure they're not very good people."

"How d'ya know?"

"The guy who came around from the back…did he say anything to you?"

"He *started* to…"

"What did he say?"

"He asked me what I wanted."

"What did you tell him?"

"I didn't have a chance to tell him anything. That's when you called and told me to split."

"He didn't say anything else?"

She shook her head.

"Did you see him do anything?"

"Like what?"

"Like pull out a cell phone."

"He had one in his hand."

"What else?"

"Whaddya mean?"

"What was his other hand doing?"

"He had it in his pocket."

"It's a good thing we got her in time," Mike said.

"Yeah…"

"Yeah what?"

I pulled out of the station, headed north for about a quarter of a mile, and pulled into the lot of a motel that was almost directly across the highway from Fieldcrest. "You have any friends or relatives close?"

"They usually hang out at the Mall in the summer."

"That's too far."

"What's too far?"

I crossed the lot, until the front of the TransAm pointed east. There were only three vehicles parked in front of the motel rooms, so I didn't think we'd have a problem with nosy visitors. I eased up to the four-foot-high concrete wall until I had a fairly good vantage point. The I stopped and switched off the engine. "Listen to me, now. I need you to sit there and stay quiet, okay?"

Her eyes immediately grew. "What are we gonna do?"

"*You're* gonna just sit there and behave yourself for once in your life. I'm gonna watch the house—just as I was doing before, when you turned stupid and nearly messed up everything."

She glanced at the binoculars. "Is that what *those* are for?"

"Good guess." I checked once again to make sure we had a good view of the street. Then I grabbed the binoculars and shifted in my seat. "I've got to see what's going on."

"You mean—"

"I told you to be quiet."

"Want me to go over there again and do another check?" Mike asked.

"That would be a really good idea."

The kid didn't question that--for whatever reason.

***

About twenty minutes later, a dark-colored sedan stopped in front of the Henderson house.

I glanced at my watch: 3:10. The car pulled up to the curb, stopped, then began backing up the drive. My angle was limited, but I could tell that as it drew closer to the house, the garage door was being raised. The sedan kept moving until it entered the garage. About ten seconds later, the front bumper cleared the doorway. I guessed that the garage door closed right after.

"Interesting," I whispered.

"What's going on?" the kid whispered back.

"I wish I knew."

"Why'd you said that, then?"

"I was thinking out loud."

"Another old person thing?"

I turned in my seat. "Don't *you* ever think out loud?"

"Once in a while…"

"Then no, it ain't exactly an *old person thing*, dammit."

"You don't have to be so *huffy* about it…"

I turned back to my binoculars. I knew it wouldn't be long before Mike came back. Once she told me what was going on, I'd have to find somewhere to dump the kid. I didn't want her with me on this and I surely didn't want her going back to her home. Judging by her previous actions, I knew I couldn't trust her to stay out of this, and I couldn't proceed with a curious fourteen-year-old sitting beside me in the TransAm, more than anxious to do something stupid. Besides, she was getting on my nerves, and I didn't want to subject her to more of my caustic charm. She'd nearly botched the whole works and I was finding it harder and harder to concentrate with her sitting right there beside me, asking stupid questions.

As it stood, I had no idea what was going on, and unless I found a safe place to stash her, I was kind of stuck between a rock and a hard place. I couldn't just take her where her mother worked and explain things to the lady; that most likely wouldn't go over very well. I had no idea what sort of person her mother was. If she was anything like her daughter, she might call the police—which, at this point, would get a lot of others involved and tear everything wide open. The fact that she worked in a bank told me nothing about her personality or how she handled things in a crisis. I only knew that she was a mother, and mothers generally turned stupid and clueless when they thought their little treasures were in danger.

"I know you can't talk." Mike materialized directly behind me. "I'm gonna say this so you won't have to ask any questions and frighten her in the process. Two people came to the house—a man and a woman. I never saw either before, but the woman was definitely the stripper the other two had mentioned. She looked just like a stripper should look—lots of long blond hair, big boobs, slender body, long legs, tight clothing. They called her Heather, and she brought a briefcase with her and some papers. The briefcase was filled with money, and there was a package in the trunk of the car everyone looked at as soon as they all met in the garage. And no, they didn't say anything about it. Paco just said it looked all right and that it should go right back out. The guy who'd come over with Heather wanted to wait until it got dark, so no one saw them taking it away, but Paco told him to shut up and do this the way it was planned. Heather also told him to shut up, and when *she* said it, it seemed to be more effective than when Paco said it. It tells me he's more afraid of her than he is of Paco—which doesn't make any sense to me, because Paco's a guy and looks pretty dangerous. And besides, Paco's friend has a gun. But what do I know? I'm dead, so I really shouldn't know anything—right?"

I shrugged.

"One other thing," Mike said. "They were talking about keeping a low profile for a few days, and Sanchez mentioned having another look around the neighborhood to see if he could find that meddling little redheaded bitch, as he referred to her. Paco didn't think there was a problem, but Sanchez said he didn't like anyone snooping around. He's afraid she saw something she shouldn't have. Paco said it wouldn't hurt anything to keep an eye out, but unless he saw her again, he shouldn't worry. But when Sanchez asked what he should do if he saw her again, Heather told him to bring her into the house, knock her out, tie her up and then drive her somewhere and dump her."

Hearing this, I knew Mike had been right when she suspected the stripper was the one in charge. But that last statement made my skin crawl. It told me Heather was not only in charge, but she was also vicious. Anyone who could order something like that done to a fourteen-year-old girl needed to be in prison.

I knew right then that there was no way I could let Tabby return home—not until this was all over.

I kept watching through the binoculars. About two minutes later, the sedan emerged, went down the drive, made a left and turned left onto Oak Ridge. I tried getting the plate number but managed only to get a couple of digits.

"It's gone," I said.

"What's gone?" the kid asked.

"A car I never saw before."

"Don't worry about following it," Mike said. "They mentioned another delivery tonight, around eight o'clock."

"Good. Then I've got time."

"Whaddya mean, good?" The kid sounded angry. "And what have you got time for?"

"I've got to take you somewhere."

"Whaddya mean?"

"What part of that didn't you understand?"

"The part about you taking me somewhere."

"Think about it for a few moments. I think you'll eventually figure it out."

"You're *taking* me somewhere?"

"You sure are quick when you really concentrate."

She ignored my remark. "Where're you taking me?"

I flicked on the engine. "I've got to find a place to hide you."

"Hide me? Why?"

"I don't want you getting into any more trouble, and I surely don't want you doing anything that'll get us killed."

***

Tabby was silent for the next couple of miles. I could tell by the tense way she sat that she was scared and confused. But just as we were about to make a left at the intersection of Oak Ridge and South Orange Blossom Trail, she turned in her seat. "*Please* tell me where you're taking me…"

"Winter Park."

"Winter *Park*?"

"As I said before, I have to find a safe place for you to stay while I take on this job."

The image of Phil, my ex-wife, flashed in my head. It seemed the perfect solution. Her condo was out of the way and in a private community. As far as I knew, no one suspected we were connected. She still went by her maiden name of Hartland, and her circle of friends could only be classified as high-profile and snobbish. And with the possible exception of a small handful of politicians, her crowd did not include anyone associated with the underworld.

"But…Winter *Park*?" She'd said it as if I was taking her to a backwoods shack somewhere in Bulgaria.

"Good. You're paying attention."

"What's there?"

"Don't you mean *who's* there?"

"Whatever…"

"A lady who just might be able to help us out."

"Who's that?"

"Oh no," Mike said. "You're talking about your ex-wife, aren't you?"

"Unfortunately."

Tabby tilted her head. "Who's Unfortunately?"

"My ex."

"You...want me to stay with...your *ex*?" Tabby asked softly.

"I think you'll be safe there."

"For how long?"

"As long as it takes me to find out what's going on and who the bad guys are."

"I dunno..."

"We might not have much of a choice, you know."

Tabby shook her head.

"What's wrong?"

A shrug. "She's...your *ex*..."

"So?"

"You mean, you two---she doesn't...hate you?"

"Not since we've been divorced."

"But...your *ex*?"

"Actually, we're good friends now."

She watched me as if she was waiting for me to tell her I was joking. When she realized I wasn't, she said, "Whaddya gonna tell her about me?"

"Phil can handle something like this."

"*Phil*?"

105

"Her real name's Felicia. I've been calling her Phil since we started going together."

"I thought maybe you *were* funny or something…"

"I already told you I didn't go that way, didn't I?"

"I guess I thought you could've been lying..."

"Why would I lie?"

She shrugged. "It's not cool to be a gay detective, is it?"

"I'm not *gay*, dammit…"

She cringed and moved toward the door.

"Actually, Phil happens to be a beautiful, classy woman. A lot of beautiful women have men's names. I also have a terrific friend named Mike who's just as much of a babe as Phil."

"You'd better stop right there…" Mike raised one of her brows.

"*Mike*?"

"She's one hot babe, too…"

Tabby thought about that for a few moments. "So…you know two ladies, they're both beautiful, and they both have *guy's* names?"

"That just about sums it up."

"What's this Mike lady do?"

"She helps me out once in a while."

"*Once* in a while?" Mike huffed. "*Please*…"

"Actually, she helps me out a lot."

"*Much* better…"

"Is she a detective, too?"

"Kind of…"

"Does she have her own agency?"

"She likes working outdoors, actually."

106

"How come?"

"She's kind of a free spirit."

"Cute," Mike said.

"And she helps you?"

"She's really good. And she doesn't ask for much in return."

"I don't ask for *anything* in return," Mike said flatly.

"I think I'd prob'ly like her," Tabby said.

"It's impossible not to."

"Now *there's* a compliment if ever I heard one..." Mike was smiling.

"Do you think she can help you with this job?"

"I'll be sure to ask for her help once I know you're safe."

"Your ex...she knows what you do for a living?"

"Of course she knows."

Mike was still smiling. "I was just thinking of some really interesting future images."

"She doesn't like it, I'll bet..."

"She hates it."

"Is that why you two split?"

"Don't get personal, now..."

"Sorry."

"Trust me. She'll be fine with this."

"Don't you think you should call her first?" Mike asked.

"Yeah. I think I'll do that."

"Do what?" the kid asked.

"I think I'd better call her first."

Tabby's eyes grew. "You haven't called her to tell her about this yet?"

"Not yet."

"You think she'll be okay with it?"

"Phil's a great lady. She won't mind it a bit." My hand shook a little as I got out my cell.

Chapter 10

I soon realized there had been no need to worry.

As I'd suspected, Phil was perfectly okay with the idea. When I first mentioned it, her immediate silence told me she was considering all sorts of activities she could share with the kid, such as watching something meaningful on *Lifetime*, engaging in charades--maybe even taking the kid with her on a spontaneous shopping spree.

Phil was a fun lady; she'd always been able to identify with all sorts of people. Her social expertise greatly enhanced her career as President and CEO of Philo-Media Consultation Services in Orlando, where she and her small staff did professional consulting for various social groups.

However, when her brief silence abruptly ended, I realized that I'd been slightly optimistic in my initial evaluation.

"How in heaven's name could you possibly think I'd be able to baby-sit a fourteen-year-old girl?" Her voice was low, but icy. Phil rarely shouted. I'd learned long ago that she didn't have to raise her voice to get her point across. Once she'd embarked on one of her quiet rampages, her tone turned venomous, and I found myself instinctively grabbing my testicles to protect them from the flames of her wrath.

But since I was driving, I couldn't grab them the way I wanted to and knew right then that I had to do whatever it took to keep her from sending her venom over through the Blue Tooth.

"It'll just be for a few hours, and it'll really help me out."

"Ralph, you know I'm not good with kids."

"This girl's not actually a *kid*…"

"You just said she's fourteen, didn't you?"

"She'll be fifteen soon."

"How soon?"

"Just a few months."

A deep sigh. "How many months, Ralph?"

I glanced at the kid. "How soon will you be fifteen?" I whispered.

"Next May," Tabby said.

"Ralph?"

I swallowed. "Not *that* many, actually…"

"I heard her, Ralph. May's almost eleven months away, last I checked."

"Phil…"

"In other words, she's fourteen."

"Going on thirty."

"Ralph, to repeat myself…you know I'm not good with kids."

"You'll be fine."

"For one thing, I'm at work."

"That won't matter. I'll just bring her over. You won't even know she's--"

"No, Ralph."

"Why not?"

"You know how I am about my place…how obsessively anal I am about my things and how everything has to be in its place, and if it's not, I actually see red…"

"She won't touch anything, Phil…" I glanced at the kid. "You won't touch anything, will you?"

She shook her head.

"See there, Phil? She said she won't touch anything."

"I didn't hear her say anything, Ralph…"

"She shook her head. Really. She's a nice girl."

Silence. She was thinking it over. When Phil was thinking something over, that's when I really got nervous. This was when she went back to her education in Philosophy and Psychiatry and used a slew of four-dollar words to analyze me and make me feel like I should be sitting in a rubber room.

"What's this really about? Is this some sort of case? Or are you in the process of adopting a child?"

"It's a case I'm working on."

I heard her sigh again and knew I was in even more trouble. When Phil began sighing, she was on the verge of hanging up. "In other words," she said, "there are very bad people involved."

"I'm not really sure, but I just don't want to take the chance—know what I mean?"

"And just what does this fourteen-year-old have to do with all this?"

"Nothing, really."

"Then why does she need protection?"

"I guess you could say she was in the wrong place at the wrong time. I don't want her to get hurt, Phil."

"Is there a mother or father in the picture?"

111

"She works in a bank. Her father's serving in Iraq."

"Why can't you just call her mother and--"

"There isn't time."

"Why not?"

"Well, because there are people watching their house, and--"

"No, Ralph."

"Listen, Phil…"

"You don't remember what happened the last time you showed up at my condo, and some *very* bad people were after you?"

"Well, actually--"

"Would you like me to refresh your memory?"

"You really don't have to bother…"

"There were bad people after you the last time you showed up on my doorstep, but that was really no surprise, because that's what you do, Ralph. It's your profession, your way of life, and it's the main reason why I left you. I loved you--I still do--but I could no longer endure you coming home severely injured, or not coming home at all. Your last visit brought everything back. In fact, it frightened me so much, I couldn't sleep for weeks. I even installed a security system and considered buying a guard dog."

"You're not good with dogs, Phil…"

"I'm better with dogs than with kids. Dogs sit there and listen to your every word. They'll love you and protect you, and as long as you keep feeding them, they'll stay with you all their life."

"Why didn't you get one, then?"

"I decided it wouldn't be fair to the dog to be there by itself all day while I'm working."

"You always did have a big heart…"

"Flattery won't work, Ralph."

"But this should be a piece of cake. Since you've got a security system--"

"No, Ralph…"

"It's all right," Tabby said behind me.

"What's that?"

"Tell her it's okay. I don't want her to be scared or anything, and I don't want her to hate you 'cause of me…"

"She won't hate me. She's just a little reluctant because--"

"Ralph?" Phil said.

"Yeah?"

"Is that her speaking?"

"Yeah…"

"Bring her over."

"What?"

"I said, bring her over."

"But you just said--"

"I know what I said."

As usual, Phil was trying to confuse me. It was frustrating to realize that she was still an expert at it even after all these years. "Why'd you change your mind?"

"She sounds grown-up and intelligent, and very ladylike."

"Are you sure, Phil?"

"I'm very good at evaluating people by hearing them speak, Ralph. Yes. I'm sure."

"Thanks."

"Now that I'm thinking it over, I figure I owe you anyway, after that huge favor you did for me a couple of years ago that nearly got you killed."

"You mean when I picked up that rich brat at the airport and spent the next couple of days looking all over town for her when she disappeared and then suddenly reappeared as if nothing happened?"

"Yes."

"That's funny. I thought you'd forgotten."

"I don't forget things like that, Ralph. But this girl sounds fine. What's her name?"

"What's your name?" I asked the kid.

"Why do you keep forgetting my name?" Her face turned red. "I must've told you a zillion times, it's—"

"It's Tabby," I told Phil.

"I take it her full name is Tabitha?"

"No one calls her that. Remember that, now."

"Just bring her on over. I'll be home around five-thirty."

"Where's the spare key?"

"In its usual place. And Ralph?"

"Yeah?"

"Once you get inside, you'll have to reset the alarm. The code is a six-digit number. Remember the day, month and year of my birth?"

"Of course I do."

"That's the code. In that order. Two digits apiece."

It suddenly bothered me that she was giving out her code so easily.

"Ralph? Everything okay?"

"You don't, by any chance, give that out to just anyone, do you?"

"You're being silly, Ralph. You know I don't like it when you're silly."

"I remember."

"He's always silly," the kid said flatly.

A pause. I could actually *hear* Phil smiling at that one. "You've got the code, right?"

"Right."

"You're sure, now?"

"I've got it, Phil. I'm not that stupid..."

"You are when you're silly."

I sighed. "I'm over it, now."

"You'd better be. If you forget or mess up, the Winter Park Police Department will be there in seven minutes or less to see what's going on. I don't want to have to bail you out of jail while I'm watching a fourteen-year-old girl."

Chapter 11

It was just before five when I pulled into one of the two guest parking spaces in front of Phil's two-story Winter Park condo. Tabby, Mike, and I got out, and we went up the two stone steps leading to her front entrance.

Half a dozen large potted plants stood in a tastefully arranged group on the sandy ground just to the right of the door. I chose the one in the center, where a faded dead leaf was poking out of the soil. A tiny brown envelope containing a spare key was clipped to the stem of the leaf. I used the key to open the front door. I immediately returned the key to its envelope, pushed it back into the soil and ushered Tabby inside with me. Mike was already inside when I closed the door. She was looking around, as usual.

The white security system box, bolted to the foyer wall, beeped softly on yellow standby. I opened it and entered the appropriate numbers. It immediately turned green and went silent.

Tabby was standing at the door, watching me. She acted like she didn't know what to do.

"She's scared," Mike said. "Make her feel at home."

"Hungry?" I asked Tabby.

"A little."

"I'm good," Mike said, winking.

I could tell she was in one of her impish moods, so I ignored her. "Let's see what we can find."

I led the way through the artfully decorated living room, down the hall past the elegant white furniture, black throw rugs, and glass-topped tables covered with modern sculpture and imported knickknacks. The place hadn't changed much, but I noticed a huge abstract painting I hadn't seen before that covered most of the opposite wall. It looked like a couple of strands of barbed wire lying on a green carpet, with twisted shreds of white toilet tissue tossed on top of the works. It was one of those godawful-looking accent pieces that probably went for a small fortune.

The place had the same familiar cigarette-and-mint mix to it. Phil used the most powerful air fresheners on the market to hide the foulness of her constant smoking, but nothing was ever quite strong enough to disguise it totally.

Mike began fading. "I'm gonna need a recharge. I'll be back shortly." Then she was gone.

"Okay."

"Huh?"

"Just talking out loud again."

The kid frowned. "You do that a lot."

"Usually when I'm thinking too much."

"Really?"

"It's my subconscious trying to tell me to tone it down and relax."

We passed a large glass ashtray sitting in the center of a shiny black end table. It was brimming with spent butts.

"She smokes a lot, doesn't she?" Tabby screwed up her nose.

"Like a freight train."

"How come?"

"It's part of her charm."

"Huh?"

"I'm just being witty again."

"You do *that* a lot, too."

"Sometimes life gets boring. Being witty's the only way I know to liven things up."

"In *your* line of work? You really think life's *boring*?"

"I'm funny that way."

We reached the large open kitchen area. Tabby climbed one of the four elegant black barstools and thumped her elbows onto the elegant granite countertop. I opened the fridge and saw right off that Phil's tastes hadn't changed. Smoked salmon, sliced roast beef, quail's eggs, and a glass dish of assorted gourmet cheeses sat on the center rack. A small fruit basket took over the lower shelf. Bottles of Cabernet, chardonnay, Gewurztraminer, and sauvignon stood in a neat row on the door shelf. A couple of bottles of Guinness on the shelf in back brought a grin to my face. I wondered if she kept those there for me. I decided they'd probably been there since my last visit.

Even so, finding something the kid would like was going to be rough. "What would you like? Try and keep it simple."

"How 'bout a sandwich and some milk?"

I didn't see any milk, but there was a can of Sprite on the door beside the Cabernet. "Sprite okay?"

"Sure."

I handed her the can and found a clean glass from the cupboard. Then I went back to the fridge, opened the freezer, and pulled out half a loaf of German pumpernickel bread. "How about pumpernickel?"

"What's *that*?"

"Dark German bread with a bunch of seeds."

"Whaddya gonna put on it?"

"Roast beef?"

She nodded.

"Mayo, mustard, or horse radish?"

"Mayo. Any cheese?"

"She's got havarti, Swiss, Monterey Jack, Limburger, and a couple of things with a hundred letters I couldn't pronounce if I tried."

"No cheese spread?"

I laughed. "You're in the wrong place for that, kiddo…"

"She's…kinda snooty, isn't she?"

"I'll have you know Phil's one of the greatest ladies I've ever known. She's bright, witty, clever, quick, and loads of fun to have at parties."

"That mean yeah?"

"Yeah, snooty's a pretty good word."

"My mom's snooty whenever some of her friends from the bank come over."

"I'll bet your dad isn't snooty, is he?"

"How'd you know?"

"I've known a few Marines in my day."

She smiled. "Dad's pretty cool."

I fixed her the sandwich, put it on a plate and slid it over to her.

She took it and looked at me. "Aren'tcha gonna have any?"

"I can't stay long. The case, remember?"

She nibbled on her sandwich, picked up her glass and washed it down with Sprite. "What do I do while I'm here alone?"

"Phil should be here shortly. In the meantime, don't touch anything."

"How can I use the bathroom if I can't touch anything?"

"Don't touch anything expensive, artsy, rare-looking, or breakable--especially breakable. You can use the widescreen—and, of course, the bathroom."

"How 'bout the stereo?"

The thought of this kid listening to Mozart made me want to laugh. "I really don't think you'll like what she's got in the console."

"I might."

"Phil's tastes lie with the classics. As you said, she's snooty. You wouldn't be interested."

A shrug.

"Ever hear of Puccini?"

"Who?"

"Shostakovich? Ravel? Tchaikovsky? Beethoven? Mozart? Brahms?"

She nodded. "I won't go near the stereo."

"I won't be long, I promise. And when she gets here, the two of you can, well, you know…"

"Know what?"

"Talk about stuff. Phil's a bright lady. She's got firsthand knowledge of tons of things. She's been to different places, knows a lot of people--"

"I'll be okay." She bit into her sandwich.

I could tell by her tone that I'd better get this job finished up quickly so I could get back before something bad happened here.

"Any chips lying around somewhere?"

I went over to the pantry and opened the door. The shelves were crammed with wine bottles, eggnog, brandy, Scotch, tins of salmon, oysters and shrimp, and paper products. There were boxes of fancy crackers, packs of rice cakes and bags of assorted chips more suited for formal gatherings than something a kid would go for.

"You don't like rice cakes, do you?"

"Yuck..."

"Bran?"

"Gross..."

"Nuts?"

"Cool."

I brought over a small bag of cashews Phil had probably taken from one of her plane trips. I dropped it on the counter.

Tabby frowned. "That's *it*?"

"For now."

She picked it up and examined it. "There're like, eight cashews in it..."

I went back to the pantry, found two more bags, and dropped them on the counter next to her glass. "There. Now you've got two full dozen to wade through. Like I said, I won't be long. How about if I bring something when I come back?"

"When will that be?"

"No idea. Maybe I can call Phil and ask her to stop on her way home--"

"No, it's all right."

"She'll probably pass a hundred different stores and 7-Elevens by the time she gets here..."

"I'll be fine. She's nice enough to let me stay here. I don't wanna be an asshole and make her go to any extra trouble."

"It won't be any trouble. And watch your language."

"She doesn't swear, does she?"

"Like a sailor when she's riled, but I wouldn't get her going if I were you. Best keep this as mellow as possible."

"I get it."

I checked my watch. It was nearly a quarter past five. I really didn't want to be here when Phil got home. I knew nothing bad would happen, but I didn't want to be delayed any longer. Mike hadn't come back yet and I knew I had to get back to that house and continue my stakeout. "I really need to leave."

"Don't worry. I'll be all right." Tabby had finished her sandwich and had a sip of her Sprite.

"I hope so. And don't forget what I said."

"Don't touch anything really cool or breakable."

"Right."

"But I'm allowed to turn on the widescreen and use the toilet..."

"Right. And don't touch any of the wines or whiskeys."

"I won't."

"You're too young to drink."

"I know."

"Good." I felt very sorry for her at that particular moment and truly hoped I could solve this case so she could go back home. "I'll do my best to get this done."

"I hope so…"

"Make sure the door's locked after I leave."

"'Kay…"

"One other thing."

"What's that?"

"Call your mom and tell her you're with a friend."

"She'll wanna know who it is."

"You told me you have friends, right?"

"A couple."

"Any of them live fairly close?"

"Marty."

"Male or female?"

"She's a girl, and she lives a couple of streets down. What do I tell my mom?"

"You're a kid. Kids have unlimited imaginations. Think of something, but whatever you do, don't tell her the truth."

"I'm s'posed to *lie*?"

"In this case? Yes. And do a good job."

She blinked. "I'm not *s'posed* to lie, am I? My dad always tells me the truth is the best way to go."

"Normally, yes…"

"Normally?"

"You can lie if the truth could cause serious harm or bodily injury to a person."

"Who'd be harmed or injured if I told the truth?"

"Me, if your mom finds out what's been going on…"

"It was *my* fault that guy saw me—wasn't it?"

"Kid, *I'm* the grownup here. *I'm* supposed to be in charge. No matter what happened, your mom'll blame *me*."

"I think I get it. I just don't know what to tell Marty."

"Tell her you're staying with a guy all day."

Her eyes grew. "She'll think—"

"I don't care what she thinks. Once this is over, you can tell her and your mom the truth. Tell your friend you're with a guy and make sure she tells your mom you're with her when and if she calls."

"What if Mom asks her to put me on the phone?"

"You've got a cell phone, right? If that happens, tell Marty to call you on your phone. Then you can call your mom right back and tell her you're okay."

She thought about that for a moment and nodded. Then she began looking confused again. "What if…what if she wants to talk to Marty while I'm on the phone?"

"Tell her Marty's in the can. Then put your mom on hold, call Marty, and have her call your mom back."

"This is sounding really complicated and messed up."

I was getting tired of all this thinking. If Mike had been here, she would've seen the signs and told me to calm down. I managed to do it on my own this time. "It wouldn't have been, if you'd listened to me in the first place and stayed away from that house."

She sighed. "Things get more complicated as you get older, don't they?"

"Wait till you're on your own and have to figure out things for yourself. This is a cakewalk."

I went outside, hurried down the walk and got back in the TransAm.

Mike appeared beside me just as I pulled out. "Is she gonna be okay?"

"I think so. She understands what's going on."

"I'm talking about her getting along with...well, you know..."

"I think they'll be okay."

"You mean you hope they will?"

"Yeah. I really and truly hope they will."

Chapter 12

We were back in the area by six-thirty.

While I parked in front of the 7-Eleven down the street from the Château DeVille on Oak Ridge, Mike drifted on over to the Henderson house. It was past dinnertime, and since I knew it would be a while before I'd be able to have time for a regular meal, I decided to stop by the store and buy some chips, dip, and a bottle of iced tea.

I went inside and quickly caught sight of a skinny blond babe in a loose-fitting faded blue sleeveless crop top, tight red shorts and open-toed sandals. She had long legs and a thick ponytail, and was bent over, staring at the beer behind the frosted glass of the refrigerator. She wore a tatt on her right forearm that I couldn't quite make out and what looked like the head of a leopard on her shoulder. She also had tatts on both legs, just above her ankles. I couldn't make them out, either. The one of her right ankle looked like a boat anchor, but I couldn't be sure. She also had something on her lower back that showed only partially because her top had slid up a couple of inches while she was bent over. It was in block letters, but I couldn't make it out without getting closer.

For a moment I'd forgotten why I'd come in, but when another equally hot babe appeared from an aisle, walked right over to the blonde and rubbed her butt, my moment of rapidly growing lust instantly evaporated, as if I'd just been doused with a bucket of ice water. Frustrated and a little embarrassed, I grabbed a chilled bottle of iced tea from the cooler and went searching for a small bag of Doritos, or sour-cream-flavored ruffled chips. Then I paid, left, and got back in the TransAm.

This time I parked on the other side of Fieldcrest, two doors down from the main drag and directly across the street from Henderson's house. It was a much shorter street, with fewer houses and only two other parked vehicles, so I couldn't risk using my binoculars as I did before. Evening rush had tapered off somewhat, but Oak Ridge traffic was still heavy. I had to limit my scans to thirty-second intervals when I was sure no one was watching.

Mike joined me just as I had my last slug of iced tea. "Aren't you afraid that'll spoil your supper?"

"This *is* my supper."

She gave me a look of disapproval.

I ignored it and munched on a potato chip. "So what's happening?"

"There are only two of them there right now—Paco and Sanchez. Paco was talking to Heather and the other guy on their cell phone. They're on the way over and should be here in about twenty minutes."

"Then what?"

"I don't know. Apparently Paco and Sanchez have to go to work, so they won't be staying in the house much longer."

"Where do they work?"

127

"They kept mentioning the club."

"Great. There are only dozens of them on the Trail."

"I don't think it'll be hard to track them down. The stripper works there, too."

"Do we know if she's working tonight as well?"

"She did say she had to get cleaned up after she makes the pick-up."

"What pick-up?"

"She's picking up a briefcase."

"What about that package?"

"I'm not sure. I think maybe Paco and Sanchez might be taking that somewhere else."

"In other words, there's a package and a briefcase. There's money in the briefcase, but we don't know what's in the package. Am I right so far?"

"Pretty much."

"And the girl and that guy with her are coming over to pick up the money while Paco and Sanchez are taking the package somewhere else?"

"Make sense?"

This sounded like the four of them were pulling some sort of scam. It also sounded like they were doing it to someone they shouldn't be messing with. "It's beginning to, but I still don't have the details I'll need to put it all together."

"How about if I go back over there and find out where Heather and her boyfriend are going and why?"

"That still leaves us wondering about those other two."

128

"And that package?"

"Yeah."

"I can't be with all four of them at the same time."

"I know. I've been meaning to talk to you about that."

She blinked. "You're not serious."

"When have you ever known me to be serious?"

"That *was* kind of silly of me."

"Extremely. But I love you just the way you are."

"Dead?"

"If it's the only way I can get you..."

"You really are sweet, you know."

"And you're being silly again."

"Sorry, can't help it. But I've got to go. It looks like someone's pulling up the drive."

"As soon as Paco and Sanchez leave, I'm going in the house and have a look around."

"That'll be dangerous, you know—especially if one of them decides to stay there."

"Didn't you hear them say they had to go to work?"

"That doesn't mean they'll both leave at the same time."

"I've got to take that chance. If something spooks me, I'll hurry back here and wait for you."

"Then you're leaving the car here?"

"I'd better. If you come back and I'm not here, check out the house."

"I'll find you, wherever you are." Then she vanished.

***

At seven o'clock, a silver Mercedes two-seater pulled up to the curb in front of Henderson's house.

With the aid of my binoculars, I saw a bosomy blonde and a tall, well-dressed guy with reddish-blond hair moving away from the sleek ride and going up the walk that led to the front of the house.

Making sure my penlight and lock-picking tools were in my pants pocket, I stuck the automatic in my jacket pocket, got out and crept down the street.

It took me about five minutes to reach the end of Fieldcrest, turn left toward Oak Ridge, sneak through the back yard separating two houses halfway down and take my position in some overgrown hedges almost directly across the street from Henderson's place. Since I couldn't bring my binoculars with me without attracting attention, I was forced to use my gut to judge when to make my next move.

I only had to wait five minutes. Before I had time to work up a serious cramp in my knees, the front door opened. The blonde and her boyfriend came out. The boyfriend was carrying the briefcase, and the two of them got back in the Mercedes. Less than a minute later, they pulled away from the curb, raced down the street and made a right at the end, which would take them back to Oak Ridge.

Although I couldn't see her, I knew Mike was somewhere in the sweet ride with them.

I went back to watching the house and waiting once again for signs of activity. This time, I had to see what Paco and Sanchez were going to do. I knew better than confront them. I also knew how dangerous it would be to let them see me. Paco, no doubt, was a thug—possibly even a strong-arm for the Mob. Sanchez was a psycho in the creepiest sense of the word. The fact that he was so attached to his gun told me the whole story.

Once again, I didn't have to wait very long. Within the next ten minutes, the garage door opened. The garage stayed dark, and what looked like a dark-colored BMW eased out of the stall, low beams on, and crept down the short drive. The garage door closed immediately. The car turned left at the end of the drive and went straight down the street, in the same direction as the Mercedes. It slowed at the stop sign at the end of the block and made a right.

Although I couldn't see if both men were in the BMW, I had to take a gamble that they'd left together. I trotted across the street, cut through the yard, and approached the house from the back yard. Before approaching the rear porch, I carefully scanned the premises. The privacy fence concealed me somewhat, and the overgrown palmettos at the corners of the house provided additional seclusion. No one was out and about. At this time of night, mostly everyone was finishing dinner or watching TV.

Sensing nothing out of the ordinary, I tried the back door. Luckily, the screen wasn't locked.

Using my tools, I opened the door, slipped inside, closed the door quietly behind me and then stood in the kitchen a full minute, my hand gripping my gun as I concentrated on the silence. When I was certain I was alone, I went down the hall and had a quick look in each room. I saw no one and heard no one, and immediately went into the master bedroom at the end of the hall.

A man obviously lived here. The closet was filled with a man's shirts and nearly two dozen expensive imported suits on wooden hangers, as well as more than a dozen pairs of imported shoes arranged in a perfect row on the floor beneath them. The Baroni, Armani and Versace labels told me this was definitely the wardrobe of someone in the upper-income bracket, most likely someone who ran his own company. There were no gaps and no empty hangers to indicate that the owner of the wardrobe had taken a few select items for a trip. This in itself could be a bad sign. Since he hadn't been seen in three days, I suspected that the man wasn't far and most likely hadn't left of his own free will.

The dresser revealed displayed underwear and argyle socks neatly arranged, designer sweaters and jeans neatly folded and stacked. A small caliber handgun lay hidden amongst the underwear in the top drawer. The gun was loaded and hadn't been fired recently.

It was time to examine the other closet, as well as the dresser on the other side of the room.

It didn't take me long to determine that a woman lived here as well. And since Mike and I kept seeing the same woman, Heather the stripper proved the most likely candidate. The dresser drawers were filled with designer bras and panties, handkerchiefs and scarves, sexy night and evening wear. This was definitely stuff a babe who danced in a fancy men's club would have as standard equipment. I also found a pair of pink handcuffs in a bottom drawer, along with a vibrator and dildo. Since most strippers catered to a man's darkest desires and would be into kink, I didn't think too much about it.

The second closet overflowed with sexy sheer negligees, bikinis and gowns, slacks, jeans, skirts, and more leather wear. There were also varieties of furs, hats, caps, and even veils arranged on the top shelf.

I got out my penlight and dropped to my knees. Shoes with six-inch stiletto heels, open-toed pumps, and knee-length leather boots lined up in a long row beneath the clothes. It only took me a couple of seconds to see something that instantly aroused my suspicions. I nudged half a dozen pairs of shoes away from the floorboard and saw it immediately. The end of the wooden strip wasn't flush with the wall, indicating a possible hiding place. I pulled out my penknife, slipped the blade between the wall and the floorboard, and pulled gently. It came out easily. I stuck the penlight between my teeth and pulled the board away from the wall.

Sure enough, a gap in the drywall, about the same height as the floorboard and at least a foot long, showed prominently. I got down lower and spotted something light in color wedged three or four inches inside. Working by feel, I discovered that it was a nylon stocking. I pulled it out carefully. It was crammed with bills. I untied the knotted end and dumped its contents onto the closet floor. Ten rolls spilled out. Some were twenties, others hundreds. There was no quick way to figure how much was scattered on the carpet in front of me. Each roll looked about the same thickness, and after a quick inspection of one roll I guessed that each contained approximately fifty bills. Using that as my guide, I estimated anywhere from twenty to thirty thousand. Either way, it was a tidy sum--too much to have been saved strictly from lap dances.

I refilled the stocking and placed it on the floor to my left. Then I went back to my examination, aiming the slender white beam of the penlight directly at the opening.

I found three more piles of nylons, each about the same size as the first. Behind them, a small metal box sat on the floor about a foot farther inside the hiding space. I pulled it out carefully and set it on the carpet in front of me. It was locked, but I was able to open it easily with my tools.

Inside were three passports, a ring of keys, two one-inch stacks of hundred-dollar bills, a key to a safe deposit box, an address book, a dozen small packets of cocaine, and a thumb drive. I also found a one-way first-class ticket for one person, in the name of Gabrielle Sanchez, for Geneva,

Switzerland, scheduled for the following evening, at 10:45 P.M.

I picked up the address book and opened it.

The list was interesting, to say the least. It was some sort of journal, with time and dates of transactions. Several intriguing names and addresses printed neatly in block letters filled three pages. One of the names listed was Arturo Vega. Another was Alvin T. Myers, a high-profile local investor whose name was often linked to organized crime in the Central Florida area, specifically drug-smuggling and gunrunning. Two other names involved OPD, and a third was frequently tied in with the County Commissioner.

The passports were in different names, all belonging to females with three different hair colors and styles. However, a close look suggested they all strongly resembled Heather in the face. Their names were Akira Meyer, Sasha Yevsky, and Gabrielle Sanchez.

I stepped out of the closet, pulled out my cell, opened it and began taking pictures.

It took me less than five minutes to photograph everything I considered important. Once I'd finished, I crawled back into the closet, replaced everything just as it was and came back out.

Mike was standing beside the bed, watching me. "Find anything interesting?"

"Yeah. How about you?"

"A lot."

It amazed me that she was able to hop into the Mercedes so easily, find out things I needed to know, disappear, and find me again.

"I'm impressed that you were able to find me so easily."

She shrugged. "It was really no trouble. I came back with them."

"With who?"

"Heather and her friend. She called him Ted."

The realization hit me hard. "You mean...they're *back*?"

She nodded. "I came in first to see if you were here. They're outside right now, unlocking the front door. You really don't have much time."

I heard their voices the moment the door opened.

Chapter 13

"I think you'd better hide."

"I think you're right."

"Quick. Get under the bed."

"Why not the closet?"

"She's a stripper."

"What does that have to do with—"

Mike gave me an impatient look. "You really want to gamble on her *not* going in there?"

As usual, Mike was right. A narcissistic woman like Heather wouldn't neglect a visit to her closet each time she came into the bedroom. And since I didn't know exactly why they'd come back, I couldn't take any chances. Even if she didn't need a wardrobe change, I had to consider the possibility that she might have returned to fetch something from her secret stash.

I immediately flattened myself on the floor and crawled underneath the bed.

Moments later, I heard them marching down the hall.

Luckily, all I found under the bed were a pair of men's slippers and a few old, dog-eared men's magazines. I pushed them out of my way and then back where they were. This would afford me additional concealment in case someone dropped something close to the bed or decided to reach for the slippers.

Mike lowered herself beneath the floor and drifted over, until she was only a foot or so away from where I lay. Only her head showed above the carpet. The effect was extremely unnerving but having her so close comforted me.

"Your phone," she said.

"What about it?"

"You'd better turn it off."

Good point. Reaching for it was awkward in my cramped position, but I managed to pull it out of my pants pocket. I brought it up to my face, found the ringer and pressed it to vibrate just as they came into the room.

"You realize how crazy that guy is," the man said as soon as they came in.

The woman went over to the closet and stopped. "Of course I know, dammit. I was there, too."

"Witt doesn't like any of this, ya know. He suspects something's in the works. So does Moreno, but I think the two of us can handle them."

"I said I was there. I see and hear the same things are you do. Witt was in my *face*, goddammit. I smelled that stupid cheeseburger on his breath. Ya know how nauseous onions smell when they're coming right out at you--especially after the moron just belched beer?"

"You shouldn't keep turning him on like that. If you didn't get him all lathered up all the time, he wouldn't get so damned close."

"He's a *guy*, dammit. It really doesn't take much. I could give him a hard-on from across the room—or on the phone. He's come in the Diamond Room more than a dozen times for a lap dance, and he always picks me."

138

"Sticking those babies in his face sure won't get him off you."

"He's a slime ball. He likes *smelling* me, for God's sake…"

"I sure can't blame him for that…"

"Keep it up, Ted. If you ever wanna get lucky again…"

"I'm just tellin' you—"

"I know what you're doing. Witt makes me ill, so don't defend him, okay?"

"We both know he's crazy, but he's also making this work."

"He's not doing this for us, you know. As long as he keeps half of the haul and Vega never finds out, he'll keep this up as long as he can. But don't forget—he's not really doing anything but keeping it quiet."

"That's pretty damn important, baby. It doesn't stay quiet? We're *all* toast."

"That doesn't give him the right to get in my face all the time." She marched into the closet and started rummaging around.

"Right now, it does. Once we're finished, then you can tell him to fuck off."

Vega. They were messing around with Vega. Now I knew what was going on. The bunch of them were going behind Vega's back and stealing from him.

This was turning out even worse than I thought.

My cell vibrated in my pocket, and my heart skipped a beat. The sudden silence suggested they'd heard it, but I told myself it was just my paranoia stepping in.

"What's that look for?" she asked from the closet.

"I think I heard something."

I watched the man's tan casuals approaching the bed. My pulse literally stopped.

No one said anything. My heart thrashed. If the man had heard it and looked under the bed, I'd have to do something. But I had no idea what I could do. I couldn't even reach for my gun for fear of either of them hearing the rustling of my windbreaker.

Mike raised herself a couple of feet then lowered herself again. "Don't worry. He's staring at the bed, but it doesn't look like he's about to bend over and look underneath."

"Hear it again?" Heather asked.

He didn't reply right off. Luckily, my cell didn't vibrate a second time. Whoever had called had apparently decided to try later.

"Naw..."

"What'd it sound like?"

"A hum."

"What sort of a hum? Like a person humming a song he doesn't know the words to? Or was it more like the humming of one of those stupid electric cars?"

"Funny, Heather. Now why the hell would I hear an electric car in this room?"

"I honestly don't know. Why would you?"

"Actually, it sounded like someone's cell phone..."

My heart skipped a beat.

More silence.

"You're hearing things. Cut it out."

"Hurry up." He turned toward the closet and my heart resumed beating. "You have stuff to do before you go back on to dazzle the evening crowd."

"I'm hurrying, dammit. Hold your water."

He came closer and stopped. He was facing the closet. The tan casuals were just a couple of feet away. Just then, he backed up and sat down on the bed. Luckily for me, the mattress was firm and didn't sag much.

I heard the sound of a lighter.

"I wish you wouldn't smoke those disgusting things in here," she said from the closet. "They stink and make everything else smell really funky. I don't like it one bit."

I caught a whiff of cigarette smoke.

He chuckled. "You like *weed*..."

"Weed's different."

"Well, I don't have any blunts right now."

"I'll get some later."

"From Paco?"

"I think we'll eventually need a different supplier."

"What's wrong with Paco? He finds some seriously good stuff."

"For one thing, he's mental," she said. "He pals around with Sanchez too much, and everyone knows Sanchez is a stone-cold psycho. Sanchez likes messing people up, but I also heard he likes killing them, too."

"You listen to too much damned gossip. If Sanchez killed people, don'tcha think he'd be in prison by now?"

"Sanchez's been with Vega for what? Ten years? Vega doesn't pick people and keep them on his payroll that long unless he's sure they're willing to do whatever he tells them to."

"Good point, but that doesn't mean he actually *kills* people..."

"Paco's no shrinking violet, either. He's been a bodyguard a long time. Bodyguards have to be crazy, too, ya know..."

"Maybe, but Paco sure knows how to get hold of some good weed."

"Maybe..."

"Admit it. You really liked that last batch..."

She sighed. "Yeah, I did..."

"Then stop slamming Paco. He's not hard to deal with. And don't forget—we need him now. We need Sanchez, too. Without them, we'd have to be moving this shit by ourselves."

She came back out of the closet, sniffing. She'd obviously had some coke from her stash.

"Ya know, baby, I can always tell when you've been crawling around on all fours. Those puppies turn red and blotchy--"

"Stop being such a horny dog." She sniffed again. "I'm not in the mood."

"Woof..."

"Funny." Another sniff.

"Good stuff?"

"Not bad. Want some?"

142

"Naw, I'm driving. Besides, I don't like messing up my sinuses."

"This stuff'll clean 'em right out." Another sniff.

"We going back now?"

"We'd better..."

A sigh.

"Something wrong?" Sniff.

"I don't think we should be doing this much longer, babe. My nerves are starting to snap. I see people looking at us all the time."

"Like I keep telling you, we won't have to. A couple more of these hauls and we can go anywhere we like. In two months, we can take that one-way trip to Australia and buy that beach house in Melbourne."

Two months. I remembered the passports. Yeah, she was using this poor schmuck and was going to hang him out to dry. I also figured she'd used Henderson the same way. A high-maintenance woman like Heather would only go after successful men. Once she'd gotten her claws into them, they immediately turned stupid and horny, and wouldn't even notice what she was taking from them. Pulling them along by their dicks was no problem for a woman like her. A man could move in no other direction.

"Can't wait," he said. "I still can't believe you want me going with you."

"Believe it, baby. You and me—that's how it's gonna be."

"Well, I've already served Kelli the divorce papers, so I'll be totally free in just a few months.

I sweetened the deal to get her to speed up the deal. I offered her the beach house on Sanibel. That, the Audi and the house, and she'll be more than ready to kick me out in a heartbeat."

Silence.

"Sweet, eh?" he asked.

"Yeah," she said. "Real sweet."

Her white spikes moved closer to his casuals, until they were touching.

"He has no idea, does he?" Mike said.

I shook my head.

Except for her slight moaning, the silence continued. The moment their kiss broke, she began sniffing again.

"Nice," he whispered.

"Woulda been even nicer without that funky cigarette breath."

More silence, more moaning.

Afterward she said: "I know we're dealing with scary dudes, baby. But like I said, I've got that covered. I'd probably already be dead if I didn't know how to get by and stay on my feet."

"Speaking of that...you wouldn't mind getting off them for just a few minutes, would you?"

"Yeah, I mind. Like I said, we've gotta go. And put out that damned cigarette."

"I'll put it out when we're outside."

"Suit yourself, but like I just said, I enjoy locking lips a lot better without the ashtray breath."

A chuckle. "I could put it out right now, if you like. I won't need it if I'm busy doing something more...well, more--"

"You're not gonna get laid right now—got it?"

A groan. "Yeah..."

"Like I said, we've gotta get back. I've gotta change, put on a bunch of sweet-smelling stuff, and earn my money. You know I'm dancing tonight, and the customers won't like it if I look like I just got laid."

"Just a quickie?"

"Use your hand. I'm outa here."

"I'll remember that the next time *you're* horny and wanna whip off a piece."

She laughed. "Like *that'll* actually happen..."

They left the room and went down the hall. A few moments later, I heard the front door slam shut. Then I heard the muffled sound of the Mercedes starting up.

Comforting silence followed.

***

Mike disappeared again.

I assumed she'd gone to make sure both had left. I crawled out from underneath the bed but didn't move until Mike came back to tell me it was safe. About two minutes after I'd heard the Mercedes start up and ebb into silence, I saw her materializing in the doorway. "You're safe. They drove away."

Relieved, I got to my feet. "I'm beginning to see what this all about," I told her. "That woman's playing with fire. She's working one helluva scam, and she's pushing a bunch of dangerous guys around to help her do it. I also think she was playing Henderson and probably got rid of him when she no longer needed him."

"You think he's dead, don't you?"

"I wouldn't be at all surprised. This other guy, Ted, is divorcing his wife because of Heather—which makes him a pathetic idiot. I can tell by what little I heard that Heather's just using him to help her with her scam. A babe like her would have no problem getting any guy to do whatever she wanted."

"I can also tell she's just stringing him along. She's really not treating him very well, is she?"

"She's leaving the country tomorrow night. I'd hazard a wild guess and say that she doesn't plan on wasting any time with good-byes."

"How'd you find that out?"

"She's got a stash hidden in her closet. Passports, money—everything she'll need to begin a new life somewhere else with a new identity."

"No one deserves being treated like that."

"Not even a guy leaving his wife for a stripper?"

She frowned. "You just raised a valid argument for being treated like that."

I pulled out my cell. The display showed Phil's number. I pressed reply; she answered on the second ring.

"I take it you were busy."

"You could say that." I'd learned long ago that it was best not to give her any details about

146

what I was working on. Phil was normally very cool and collected, but it didn't take much to get her back on a regimen of meds. That wasn't my main concern now, but I knew better than tell her anything else--for her sake, as well as for the sake of the kid. "How are you and the kid doing?"

"Her name is Tabitha, and we're doing just fine."

I heard the kid yell, "*Tabby!*" in the background.

"Whatever."

I heard the kid say, "Did he just say whatever?"

"That he did."

I suspected something strange was going on. Phil had always been much too career-minded to think about raising kids and had never been the maternal type. But I was relieved they were getting along. "She hasn't broken anything or drugged you, has she? I'm visualizing the place overrun with a hundred of her friends getting stoned, raiding the refrigerator, running around, and jumping all over the furniture."

"Can you hear *anything* that might sound remotely like that going on right now?"

"No..."

"Don't be silly, then. She's a very well-behaved young lady, and I'm ashamed of you for even thinking such a thing."

"What'd he say?" Tabby asked in the background.

"Nothing worth mentioning, dear." Phil turned away from the phone. "He's just trying to be funny."

"He does that a lot, doesn't he?"

"Entirely *too* much."

"Want me to hang up so the two of you can finish discussing my shortcomings without my actual contributions to the conversation?"

"Actually, it would take entirely too long to discuss all of your shortcomings."

"Ouch."

"You deserved that and you know it."

"I guess I did. I'm sorry, Phil. I guess I misjudged her..."

"We're having a very pleasant visit. She's showing me her artistic talents."

"She's *artistic*?" Somehow, the idea surprised me.

Phil groaned. "Why'd you say it like that?"

"Like what?"

"Substitute the word "contaminated" for "artistic" and you'll get the full impact of the image you just sent over."

"Er, sorry again. I guess I *have* misjudged her. So...what's she doing?"

"A sketch."

"Of what?"

"Me."

"You?"

"We're in the living room, and I'm in my robe, relaxing."

I heard the kid cough.

"And smoking, of course."

"*I'm* smoking. She isn't."

"I'm certainly glad of that. And you're letting her *sketch* you?"

"You're making this sound, well, obscene, somehow…"

"I know you, Phil. I just figured you to be much too shy to have anyone do a sketch of you."

"Normally I'd say yes, I am. But she's got a lot of natural talent. When I first gave her my sketch pad, she immediately did some cartoon characters, and they were simply fantastic. She also did caricatures of Clint Eastwood and Charles Bronson, and they're absolutely amazing."

"Clint and the Chucker? I'm impressed. She's definitely got my undying love and devotion."

"I knew that would get your attention."

"He likes Clint Eastwood and Charles Bronson?" the kid asked.

"He'd have their baby if he could," Phil replied flatly. "In a New York second."

"*Yuck!*"

"I'm glad you two are having such a good time. Now I don't have to worry about sending over the SWAT team for a raid."

"You actually thought you had to worry?"

"I didn't know…"

"Who were you worried about, Ralph? Me? Or Tabby?"

I didn't reply.

"All right… Now that you've officially insulted me…"

"Don't get tense, Phil. I've got a lot on my mind."

149

I heard Tabby say, "Ask him if he found out anything about my neighbor."

"I'm supposed to ask you if--"

"Tell her I'm still working on it."

"Have any leads?"

"A couple."

"Can you say what's going on?"

"I'd rather not."

She lowered her voice. "Is it looking good?"

"It's too soon to tell. I'll keep you posted."

"Be careful, Ralph."

"I will."

"And don't worry about her...or me."

"I won't." I hung up.

"What now?" Mike asked.

"We've got to find out where those two went."

She shrugged. "They're going to the Royal."

"Is that what they said?"

"They stopped by the other place before they came back. They dropped off the briefcase and came right back so she could get a change of clothes."

"So...it's the Royal, then..."

"That's where she works as a dancer."

I was impressed. The Royal was one of the most prestigious strip clubs on the Trail. It was a large, fancy place, with a giant lot, a well-maintained lawn, palm trees, and a parking lot that would rival Walmart. The property was owned by Arturo Vega. It was rumored that he used his own men to run the place but kept his involvement in the activities private.

"Since they kept mentioning Vega, I guess I should've known."

"Well, now you know for sure."

Something Mike said a moment ago began worming its way into my noggin. "Heather has another house?"

"She's keeping a few things there that might interest you."

"Sounds intriguing."

"It is, believe me."

"Can you remember how to get back there?"

"Of course."

"Great. Then all I have to do is check it out and see what's going on. Then maybe we'll know exactly what Heather and her team of horny dogs has been doing."

"There are others watching the place."

"*Watching* the place?"

"They were there when Heather, Ted and I got there."

"This tells me something bad is going on. Do you have any idea who those other guys are?"

"No, but they looked Latino."

"How many are there?"

"Two. And, of course, Paco and Sanchez."

"Paco and Sanchez?"

"They brought over the package."

"Did they stay?"

"They're still there, as far as I know."

"Ever find out what was in it?"

"I didn't have time. Heather and her boyfriend were only there two minutes. I figured

I'd better come right back with them and tell you what was going on."

"Then Paco and Sanchez are still back there, guarding things?"

"Yes. And they're heavily armed."

"Of course they are."

"But we're still going there, right?"

"You know better than ask me that."

Mike sighed. "I guess I forgot who I was talking to for a moment…"

Chapter 14

North of 192, several blocks of one-story ranch homes sit in quiet solitude off Michigan Avenue, just a stone's throw from the endless rows of fast-food places, gas stations, gift shops and shopping malls that had taken over the main drag connecting Kissimmee with St. Cloud.

Mike instructed me to turn right on Michigan, which took us north. Three streets up, I turned left, and we went down a stretch of attractive homes sitting on well-maintained lawns separated from one another by palmettos, palms, and trimmed bushes. About three-quarters of the way down the street, I turned right, and we went down two more streets.

"Turn here," she said.

I turned right; we eased down the block. About halfway down, Mike pointed to our left. "That's the place."

As I crept past the house, I caught sight of the dark sedan sitting in front of the garage. I took the TransAm past a few more houses, pulled over to the curb and parked next to a large palmetto bush at the corner of someone's yard, just beyond the driveway.

The house in question appeared no different from its neighbors. Painted a neutral tan, it boasted a small front porch, a vine-covered trellis on the far side and a long line of untrimmed bushes spanning the front, beneath the living room window and two smaller windows. Large shrubbery sat at each corner of the lot, obscuring a portion of the house from view. The grass hadn't been mowed in about a week or so but the property didn't appear to be abandoned.

From where I'd parked, I was confident no one could see the TransAm through the palmetto bush.

"Tell me what's going on in there."

"I'll be right back." Then she vanished.

Less than two minutes later, she reappeared beside me.

"That was fast."

"It doesn't take long to see two men staring at a bunch of boxes stacked in the garage."

"Paco and Sanchez are both in the garage? Staring at boxes?"

"Paco's talking on his cell. Sanchez is jumpy and keeps leaving the garage to go look out the windows."

"Any idea who Paco's talking to?"

"The guy named Witt we heard mentioned in the bedroom."

"And?"

"Paco asked for a time, and Witt said he was going to try and get someone out there before midnight. Paco didn't like that. He said he couldn't stay here that long because he had to be back at the club by ten, and if he wasn't there, the bosses would want to know where he was."

"I take it they don't want Sanchez there by himself?"

"Witt said no but didn't say why."

"Witt might not trust him. We both saw how he reacted when he saw the kid coming over to the house. Since he and Paco are obviously protecting contraband at this place, he'd be even more protective."

"That could be very bad."

"So what sort of packages are we talking about?"

"They're all the same--about the size of a square ottoman."

"You couldn't tell what's in them?"

"They're all wrapped tightly and taped up."

"With what?"

"It looked like aluminum foil, with shrink-wrap covering the works."

This was getting better by the second. "And you say the garage is filled with them?"

"The packages are stacked four high."

"How many do you think are there?"

"I didn't count them. Want me to go back there and do a count?"

"Just give me a rough estimate."

"I'd say there are about five rows of four or five, and since they're stacked four high--"

"Damn... That makes it between eighty and a hundred."

"You took all the fun out of that."

"Sorry. My mind sort of took over and went apeshit."

Mike looked puzzled. "I don't recall that happening before."

"It only happens when I get excited."

"Remind me never to get you excited again."

155

I grinned. "I could say something really crude about that."

"On a serious note…what do you think is in the packages?"

"It's either weed or coke. Or both."

"You mean they've got a garage half-filled with *drugs?"*

"Yes, Mike. I think we can safely classify weed and cocaine as drugs…"

"How do you know for sure?"

"Drugs are always covered in foil and shrink-wrap. There's nothing else I can think of that could explain what's going on here."

"Whatever would possess them to get involved in something like this?"

"I'll stretch my imagination a bit and say this is probably Heather's gig."

"But why? She obviously makes a ton of money dancing…"

"It's probably not enough."

"How much is enough?"

"For her? A pampered, high-maintenance bitch like her is usually impossible to satisfy in more ways than one."

"Where do you think they're getting these drugs?"

"Vega's got a solid pipeline coming in. From what I've heard, there are trucks coming up from Miami, and a small portion of them seem to be vanishing before they can reach Jacksonville. Vega's the only one in the Central Florida area powerful enough to handle something like that. Heather obviously got wind of it and concocted a scheme to shave a little off the shipments without anyone noticing. All she had to do was find a couple of schmucks and sweet-talk them into going along with the plan."

"You think Henderson was one of them??"

"I think Heather was looking for the perfect schmuck—successful, horny and generous. Henderson went to the club one night, saw her, and wanted her, big-time. Heather, like all gold-diggers, can sniff out a cash cow as easily as a dog sniffing out red meat. Once she found him and dug her claws in, she decided to use him to help with her plan."

"We still don't know what she needed him for."

"Well, we know for a fact that she moved in with him. This gave her a perfect place to hide her stash for her final farewell trip."

"You think that's all she wanted from him?"

"That's hard to say. She's obviously a complicated babe, so I'm sure she had a reasonably complicated scheme worked out. Once she'd assembled enough players, she gave them all a specific job. Paco and Sanchez pick up and deliver, and then there's Witt and that other guy, Moreno. She's probably using ol' Teddy-boy for some other odd jobs. These idiots are in way over their heads. They're stealing from the big guys, bringing over weed and coke and the cash that accompanies each shipment, a little at a time, and stashing it here."

"And you're positive this is Vega's stuff?"

"Vega owns and runs this area. No one would be stupid or arrogant enough to go against him without knowing the consequences."

"Vega probably also has a place of his own to keep all this stuff. That's probably how he stays under the radar."

"I'm sure Vega has several stash pads in town. It all depends on how big his operation is. He needs to have everything spread out in case the cops get wind of anything. He obviously has no idea what this bunch has been doing. He probably has just two or three of his most trusted people handling these shipments. He'd never trust anyone else to share such valuable information about his operation. I'm sure he doesn't even tell his own daughter Martina half of what he does. Vega's very old-fashioned. Women are strictly second-class with men like him. They take care of the house and the kids and give him sex whenever they're told."

"That sounds barbaric."

"Like I said, he's old-fashioned. Getting back to this… You said Paco and Sanchez are watching the place. Was anyone else in that house when you were in there?"

"I didn't see anyone."

"Then Paco and Sanchez made their drop-off and are just waiting."

"You mean they're expecting someone to show up to relieve them?"

"It actually sounds like a good plan. They'd have to spell one another every so often. This way, everyone stays alert, and unless one of them acts stupid or pulls a boner, no one in the neighborhood would suspect anything suspicious. Of course, this means more people could be involved, but if Heather's as smart as we think, she might just pay two or three guys a couple hundred apiece to watch the place without telling them why. Anyone needing extra cash would jump at the chance and not ask questions."

"I heard one of them mention another shipment coming in two days. Are you sure you're right about Heather leaving tomorrow night?"

"Positive."

"Then you really think Heather thought all this up on her own?"

"I'm just guessing, of course, but I'd say that someone like her would easily be able to devise such an elaborate scheme, using as many guys as she could find for the grunt work. This way, she'll stay out of the picture when everything suddenly goes bad. There'll be too many others stumbling about in the process, making things really complicated. I'm sure that's why she's got her early vanishing act scheduled. She probably has enough money saved and wants to get out while the going's good. She doesn't want to take any chances that Vega will get wind of what she's doing. Once that happens, she knows her days will be numbered."

"But if something *does* go bad, this Ted guy—as well as the others-- won't get away alive."

"Probably not."

"You don't think you should warn him about what's going on?"

"He wouldn't believe me. She's got her claws into him much too deep. He became a walking dead man the moment she first smiled his way."

"But what about this operation? Aren't you obligated to report it?"

"Vega will eventually smell something going on. Once these guys are discovered and caught, it won't be long before their body parts are dumped somewhere or sold as bait in the fish and tackle shops in the area."

"That's awful."

"That's what happens when you cross these mob guys. Papa Joe would do the same thing. I have no sympathy for this woman. She organized this for her own personal gain and doesn't care what happens to anyone else."

"Are you going to turn her in?"

"I have no proof—not legally— that she's tied into this. I have this feeling that even if I got the Feds here right now, she'd squeeze out of it."

"And you can't very well call Vega and tell him, right?"

"I'm a private eye, not a snitch for the Mob."

"What about that job you did for Papa Joe last year?"

"Papa Joe was a paying customer. With him, all I did was find out who was operating behind his back and sabotaging his operation."

"Isn't that being a snitch?"

"If I picked only honest people to deal with, I'd be out of business in a week. There just aren't that many honest people who need the services of a private eye."

"But what about this stash pad thing?"

"It's a highly illegal drug operation and subject to Federal prosecution. I'm obligated to report it to the local police department."

"You sound like you don't want to."

"If I ass around long enough and Vega finds out about it, innocent people could get caught in the crossfire. The pad's located in the middle of a subdivision. Whenever criminals are fighting among themselves, innocent people tend to get in the way."

"So what *are* you going to do? Call your rude policeman buddy and tell him about this place?"

"Neil would skin me alive if I called him at this hour. I've got to find out about Henderson first. Once I know what's going on, I'll give Neil a call."

"I hope no one comes over and empties the garage while we're looking into this."

"You would've heard about it when you were in the house. I think we're safe for tonight. Tomorrow could be a different story."

Chapter 15

At nine o'clock, the parking lot of the Club Royal for Men was almost packed.

Groups of well-dressed men in their thirties and forties strolled down the winding sidewalk that led to the brilliant front entrance of the huge three-story stucco building.

Nearly five acres in size, the property had been tastefully cleared of debris and overgrowth in an effort to make it look more appealing. Palm trees and palmettos sat smartly in strategic sections, with plants and flowers carefully arranged in neat rows in front of the building. The grass bordering the building was also kept up, giving the place an aesthetically natural appearance.

I parked two rows down from the front and at the far end, near a cluster of palmettos. For the next ten minutes I sat silently, watching the entrance, where a huge, dark-featured gorilla guarded the door and gave access to those handing over their ten-dollar cover. I wanted to go inside and do my shtick but didn't exactly know how to go about it. Since I didn't know what I was looking for, I knew I'd be forced to use more finesse than usual. This didn't go well with me because I didn't like using finesse. When you stuck finesse into the picture, people didn't respond the way you wanted them to, and you didn't get the reactions or the answers you were looking for.

But I had no choice. I had to keep in mind that this job was all about finding a man who might very well be dead. If this was the case, my chances of finding him were pretty close to zero. I might bump into someone who knew the man, but even that was a stretch, and unless I fabricated some sort of bizarre story, I'd end up with nothing. I also ran the risk of being seen by the wrong people. Many of Vega's people knew about me or had at least seen me before, and if any one of them spotted me, their suspicions could easily get me thrown out or detained. I could be taken to one of the offices and asked why I was asking questions or ushered outside and asked in a more direct—and in this case, physical—manner why I was making a nuisance of myself. I had an idea what Heather and her friends were doing but I couldn't voice my suspicions without endangering my life. And since I couldn't let anyone know what I was doing, I'd have to rely on Mike's special skills once again to help me with this investigation.

"You're awfully pensive."

"I know."

"It isn't like you."

"Are you saying I'm not the pensive type?"

"I'm saying it isn't like you."

"You just repeated yourself."

"I guess I did."

"I wish you'd tell me what you're thinking."

"I'm thinking that you're very uncomfortable right now. You're also confused, and don't know what to do."

As usual, Mike knew exactly what was going on.

"Mind telling me how you know that?" I asked.

"I know you. In fact, I probably know you better than you know yourself."

"Maybe, but what specifically are you talking about?"

She shrugged. "Nothing much…just that you don't like relying on anyone else for answers. You want to go in there and get everyone stirred up, but in this case, you'll get tossed out or much worse. In other words, you can't do what you'd really like to do, and it's bothering you."

It scared me that she could get into my head so easily. "You *do* know everything about me, don'tcha?"

"Being dead has its perks…"

"Obviously."

"So forget about all that ego crap that's dragging you down and tell me what you want me to do."

"I need you to go in there and sniff around."

"What am I looking for?"

"I want you to check out the executive offices and pay attention to what's being said."

"Does it matter who's saying it?"

"I'd prefer you try the club manager, but since I have no idea who the club manager is, any one of them will do."

"Maybe he'll have a *MANAGER* nametag pinned to his jacket."

"That would be helpful, but don't count on it. You might not need to know who he is if he's where he's supposed to be, so check the room marked Manager and go from there. Who knows? You might just get lucky."

"And you want me listening to anything that sounds important?"

"Focus on keywords, such as Henderson…or missing tallies…or late shipments…or anything about Heather or Paco. In other words, anything that might deal with Heather and her group of stooges. I'm going in, too, so I won't be far away."

"What'll you be doing?"

"Guy stuff. Asking about the girls."

"You're gonna try and find out about Heather in that place?"

"Exactly. Why? You sound…well, skeptical."

"I just don't think you'll be able to do this without anyone getting suspicious."

"Guys talk about babes all the time. It's part of our nature. Maybe I'll even hear something about Henderson."

She shook her head.

"What's wrong?"

"I never understood guys when I was alive, and I still don't, even though I'm dead."

"You just said you understood *me*, didn't you?"

"I'm talking about *guys*."

"What am I? A kangaroo?"

"Guys in general. You know what I mean. When guys get together—that kind of thing. Girls just don't understand. It's like you speak a different language."

"You're a female. You're not supposed to understand. We've got this mutual thing we've had going on for centuries."

"You mean acting stupid? Arrogant? Silly? Nonsensical? Childish?"

"Yeah. That kind of thing."

"I always thought it was my imagination."

"It's just guys getting together and acting like boys without being judged."

"Being judged? By who?"

"By girls—who else?"

She thought about that for a few moments and then nodded. "Well, I hope you find out about her. But like I said, I have my doubts."

"So do I, but I've got to try."

"You know there'll be more than one blond stripper in there, don't you?"

"The place is probably crawling with them."

"In the meantime, I'll find out what I can."

"I'm sure you'll accomplish more than what I'll be able to do."

"You'll be here when I come back out?"

"If I'm not, it probably means I've messed up and they've taken me somewhere to interrogate me or dump me in a lake."

"That doesn't give me a warm fuzzy, you know."

"It's the best I can do. There are some seriously scary guys in there."

She didn't say anything for the longest time. I could tell she didn't like any of this. "*Please* don't do anything stupid in there."

"I'll try not to."

"Not good enough…"

"All right. I promise I'll be as careful as I can."

She smiled. "Now *that's* what I wanted to hear."

Then she vanished.

***

After locking my .380 in the glove box, I got out of the TransAm, locked the door, and went down the walk that led to the front entrance of the big building.

I handed over my ten-dollar cover to the gorilla blocking the door and followed a group of six well-dressed guys in their forties jabbering away in Spanish and giggling stupidly when the hostess smiled at them the moment we came in.

The main room fluttered erratically with blinding, pulsating neon. Assorted masses of glossy-eyed humanity filled the huge room. Harried waitresses ignored playful swats and pats while carrying silver trays topped with drinks to their assigned tables. Laughter and drunken jeering rose above the unpleasant syncopated thumping coming from the juke. Bosomy, half-naked dancers performed provocatively from tabletops and various sections of the bar.

I went right over to the twenty-foot-long, L-shaped bar and ordered a bourbon and ice, then made my way down the carpeted hall, where square metal stands advertising the lap dancing areas posted every twenty feet or so guided my way. A huge mass of flesh in a dark, ill-fitting suit blocked the passageway where the large image of a diamond perched above the lap dancing stand. The mass sported a black brush cut, had small black eyes and the face of a pit bull gazing hungrily at me as if I were a bait dog.

"You gotta card?" it asked in a raspy low-pitched whisper.

"I've got all kinds of cards," I told its black bow tie while straining my neck. "I've got MasterCard, Visa, and even my driver's license—although I don't really like giving it out. The picture's just plain awful. It makes me look dead—or like I just ate too many enchiladas. What card will get me in there?"

"Diamond."

"A *diamond* card? What's that?"

"If I gotta tell ya, you ain't got none," it explained.

I wanted to ask it if it ever paid attention in grade school English class but decided against it. I had the strong feeling that saying something like that would probably get me killed or mauled. My enchilada remark probably didn't score too many points, either. The mass's taut expression, as well as its awesome size, discouraged any sort of levity here. Besides, I came to find out a few things—not get snatched up like a football and tossed out on my ass.

"Just one question?" I hoped it would tell me where I could get a diamond card.

A huge, cigar-sized index finger nearly put out my eye as the arm the size of a tree trunk shot out, pointing to the direction in which I'd just come.

I nodded. "Thanks. I guess that's the answer I was looking for." Then I turned and went back down the hall.

I turned the corner and joined another group standing outside a curtain a few feet from the sign, "Lap Dancing." Since there were no gems or any other markings above the metal stand, I figured it was okay for a regular customer like myself to check it out. If I was right in my assumptions, Heather was probably one of the "Diamond" dancers, available only to the more important, affluent customers. But since I obviously couldn't make any headway there without losing my head or a bunch of my favorite body parts in the process, I had no choice but check out another room. I just hoped Mike was making better progress in the executive offices.

I walked up to a small group of guys arguing about the direction the stock market was heading. One of them turned to me and said, "You an investor?"

"Do I look like one?"

He shrugged. "Who's to say, nowadays?"

"Actually, I can't afford it," I said. "You guys come here often?"

The guy beside him said, "Every chance we can."

The guy next to him said, "Best babes in town dance here."

The first guy was obviously more concerned about my financial path than the babes we were going to see. He said, "You'd be surprised. The way it's been falling, you oughta rush right in and buy a coupla hundred shares, especially software. A lot of them are gonna be penny stocks before too long."

I wanted to tell him I'd rather stick an upholstery needle into my left ear rather than mess up my finances that way.

"I wouldn't go with software," the third guy said. "Mel, here, just comes here to find new clients."

"I wouldn't mind getting laid, either," Mel said, chuckling.

"Good luck with that," the second guy said. "These dolls belong to the club. You're better off trying to score at Vesper's."

"Most of 'em suck big-time," the third one muttered, shaking his head.

"The babes?" I asked. "Or stocks?"

The three of them laughed.

The second guy said, "Both, actually. What good's a babe if you can't even touch her?"

"That doesn't stop you from going in there with a wad of five's an inch thick, Hector," Mel said.

Hector shrugged. "Doesn't hurt to keep on trying, does it?"

"I know a hedge fund guy," I said. "He does pretty well, but I still can't see myself tossing away my money like that."

"It's invested," Mel said, "not tossed away."

"I can't pull it back out whenever I want, right?"

"That's why you invested it," he said. "You don't invest money you need."

"I need ever penny I have," I said.

"Then you shouldn't be investing at all," the second guy said.

"Thanks," I said. "I guess you talked me out of it."

No response.

The third guy laughed and said, "Drop the stock talk shit, Melvin. We came here to get a lappy—not discuss tossing our money away."

"Whaddya think a lappy is, Artie?" Mel said, and they all laughed.

"You guys got a favorite dancer?" I asked.

"Lolita," Artie said.

"Roxie," Mel said.

"Ava," from Hector.

"Anyone ever see Heather?"

Silence. They all stared at me as if I'd just told them a joke and suddenly forgot the punch line.

"Too pricey," Hector said, scowling. "She's a diamond dancer. You can't even get near her."

"Hell, no," Artie said. "Bitch walks around with one of those damned Sherman tanks with no neck wearing a baggy suit. You look at her the wrong way? You get an ugly face from Sherman himself."

"How can you tell?" Artie asked, and they laughed.

"The hedge fund guy I know must be doing fairly well," I said. "He's dating her."

"Heather?" Artie asked.

I nodded.

"You sure?"

"He told me he was…"

More laughter.

"I guess I need to manage a hedge fund," Artie said.

"I'm dating Jennifer Aniston," Hector said, giggling.

"Whaddya doing here, then?"

Hector shrugged. "Everyone needs a break once in a while."

"From Jennifer Aniston?" Mel asked.

"What the hell are you?" Artie asked. "Nuts? Or gay?"

Hector giggled again. "I lied…"

More laughter.

"So no one has actually seen this Heather dance?" I asked.

"She's a diamond babe," Mel said. "For that you need to buy a card. Last I heard, they go for five grand."

"That's only for a year," Artie added.

"Just for a diamond card?" I asked.

"And also for the privilege of going in there and handing over a couple of hundred bucks each and every time you plant your ass down and have one of those babes lather you up."

"What a deal," I said.

I suddenly noticed two men standing close behind me. I hadn't noticed them before and wouldn't have been suspicious if they hadn't been standing so close. A quick glance told me they were both around forty and dressed in drab suits. Since this was Florida, I was used to crowds; I just didn't like people getting too close.

"You can spend just as much cash in this room," Mel said, "and the babes are just as sexy."

"What's the difference, then?" I asked and caught one of the men behind me moving alongside me. He stood about two feet away and was staring straight ahead, but I could tell he was listening to our conversation. The guy with him stayed behind me. I was beginning to feel trapped.

"Not much," Hector said. "I heard the diamond girls are owned by the management."

"You're full of it, Hector." Artie shook his bald head.

"I said I *heard* it. That doesn't mean I *believe* it."

"Why'd you say it, then?"

"It sounds like it could be true."

"They're *all* owned by the management, you idiots," Mel said. "It's just that the diamond girls have been hand-picked by the club's most elite customers."

"Like who?" I asked.

"That hedge fund guy you know," Mel said. "He probably owns a piece of this place."

A bouncer almost as big as the first one I'd encountered appeared from behind the curtain to let six customers slip through.

"I think we might be able to help you out," the guy beside me said in a soft voice. I casually turned and saw that the second guy was still standing directly behind me.

My paranoia raised red flags.

"Help me out how?" I asked.

"You've got a lot of questions," the man said behind me.

"I've always been the sort of guy who asks a lot of questions. I guess I can't help it. I'm an inquisitive guy. I've been asking questions all my life."

"That's why we think we can help you out," the first guy said.

Mel, Artie, and Hector were no longer listening. They'd moved up to the curtain and were eagerly awaiting their turn.

"That's all right," I said. "Once I get in there for one of their lap dances, I don't think I'll really be in the mood to care about which girl is in the diamond room and which isn't…"

"It's not about the girls," he said, and I felt something poking me in the small of my back.

My paranoia had already switched to the beginnings of panic.

I began wondering if I could spin around, chop him in the side of his neck and get away before the other guy nailed me. I also wondered if I should just toss what was left of my drink in his face. That was the problem with a situation like this. I had to consider both were armed, but I had no idea how fast they'd be. They were both around my age, but that didn't tell me anything else. The cheap suits told me just that they had lousy taste in clothes. I knew of guys my age or older who were professional bodybuilders and guys my age or older who were karate instructors. I even knew of two professional hit men who were pushing fifty, and still demanded a quarter of a mill a hit.

All I knew about these two was that the man standing behind me had what felt like a gun pressed against my spine. It didn't take a rocket scientist to realize that squeezing a trigger took much less time than spinning around and giving a guy a sharp chop to the side of the neck, or tossing my drink in his face.

But I'd been in this profession a long time and had been in this same situation several times before. If anything, it taught me to play it out and not do anything stupid.

"What's it about, then?" I asked tensely.

"It's about doing what you're told," the man behind me whispered.

The first guy moved closer, and I could feel both of them checking me out for firearms. I was relieved for not bringing my gun inside, but also cursing myself at the same time for not bringing my gun inside.

"What's the problem?" I asked, trying not to appear as terrified as I really was.

"There won't be one," the first guy said, "if you do as we say."

I shrugged. "Then say something, and I'll see if I can do it."

The gun behind me nudged me harder.

"Outside," the first one said. "And no funny business."

I had no choice. I did as they said.

Chapter 16

As soon as we stepped outside, the first guy led me down the walk, where my car was parked. We went right over and the guy behind me said, "Get in."

I knew right then that these two had recognized me. The walk straight to the TransAm was a dead giveaway. I couldn't place either of them, but I could tell they weren't Hispanic. There were a few employees in the Royal who weren't Hispanic, but somehow I had the strong feeling this was something other than a simple mugging or roughing up once we left the property. The cheap suits suggested that they could be cops, and their brush cuts told me they might be Feds.

"We don't have all night."

I reached into my pocket, pulled out my keys and unlocked the door. I got in and hoped Mike would be out shortly and work some of her magic if I needed her help.

As soon as I got behind the wheel, the first guy said, "Unlock the other door."

I reached across the seat and did as he said. For a moment I considered flipping open the glove box and grabbing my gun, but I didn't think I'd need it, and even if I did, I wouldn't be able to get to it quickly enough. Then I remembered that I'd locked the glove box—which made the notion of grabbing the gun quickly even more hilarious. As soon as I unlocked the door, the two of them got right in, one right beside me, the other in the back seat directly behind me.

I was a sitting duck.

"Now what?"

"Drive."

"Where?"

"We'll tell you when the time comes."

I eased out of the space and went up the paved road that led to the entrance. "Any direction in particular?"

"Make a right," the guy beside me said.

I did as he said, and we were soon heading south on the Trail.

"You're okay," Mike said, and I could see her smiling face as she materialized close beside me. "I got your back."

I returned her smile.

"Something funny?" the guy next to us asked.

"Just life and its endless list of surprises."

He grunted but said nothing.

"Nice night," I said, hoping to ease the tension. "Not too muggy, and the mosquito population seems to be—"

"Shuddup."

So much for easing the tension...

We went about a mile in silence. Then the guy beside me said, "Pull into the next strip mall before the light."

"We're going shopping?" I asked. "You should've told me. I didn't bring any of my gift cards or coupons."

"You're a real comedian."

"I try really hard, sometimes."

"You ever get any positive response?" the guy behind me asked.

"It depends on the crowd."

"Howzat?"

"The smart ones in the crowd usually laugh. The others are too stupid to know what I'm saying."

Mike laughed.

"You're a real smartass," the guy behind me said.

"Your partner just said I was a real comedian."

"You're both."

"Thank you. I'm pleased you think I'm so versatile."

When I pulled off the main drag, the guy beside me said, "Drive over to that sedan and park."

I took the TransAm over to a swimming pool accessories store. There were only two other vehicles parked in the small lot. All the stores were closed. A few lights were on; the streetlamp behind us cast some haze on the sedan and the bushes separating the lots. As soon as I parked and switched off the ignition, the man sitting beside me said, "Now...do you wanna tell us what you were doing at the Royal?"

"You were in the same line I was. I was looking for a lap dance—what do you *think* I was doing?"

He shook his head.

"I don't think that's what they wanted to hear," Mike said.

"Do we need to ask you again?" the guy beside me asked.

"Do I need to speak slower?"

"Yeah," the guy behind me said. "A real smartass."

"They warned us, didn't they?" The guy beside me glanced at his partner.

"Let me guess. You're undercover."

"He's good," the guy behind me said.

"Haversack told us he was."

"Neil actually said I'm *good*?" I couldn't believe it.

"He didn't come right out and *say* it," the guy behind me said.

"What *did* he say?"

"He just said that you could crack cases that seemed totally impossible to crack."

"Fancy that," Mike said. "Your rude friend *likes* you."

"Yeah," I said. "Fancy that."

"So what were you really looking for?" the first guy asked.

"What gave me away?" I asked. "And how'd you find me?"

"We've been staking out the Royal the last two months," the first guy said.

"We've seen you with Haversack a few times," his partner added.

"Did he look angry?"

The first guy huffed. "He's always pissed about something."

"Strange. I thought I was the one who brought that out."

"Let's get back to the business at hand," the first guy said, sounding a little impatient. "You were asking about one of the strippers."

"That place has got a lot of strippers. Like I said before, what gave me away?"

"And like *we* said, we've seen you before," the guy behind me said. "And you were asking about the right one."

"Heather."

The first guy nodded. "We've been trying to get close to her so we can keep an eye on her, but in this place, that's like trying to walk right up to the President without getting arrested."

"Apparently she's one of the club's biggest draws," I said.

"Obviously. One of our CI's told us she could be involved in something, well, something we really need to get a handle on."

"I take it you're working a parallel case."

"We're trying to find leads for several stash pads in the area," the first guy said. "There's been entirely too much traffic coming up from Miami, and we need to find out where the sources are. We've heard rumors about possible dump points, but after two months, we still haven't come across anything substantial."

"Care to share anything?" his partner said.

"I can take you to one of them right now."

Silence.

"You *found* one of Vega's stash pads?" The first guy perked up.

"I found one that's being operated by at least four of his people in a skimming operation.

Heather's involved, by the way. I'm pretty sure Vega's in the dark about it, but I can't say how long it'll stay this way."

"You're sure about this, Deacon?"

"Positive."

"Vega just found out about it," Mike said. "He's questioning one of the men as we speak."

"How'd you find out?" the guy behind me asked.

"You honestly want me to reveal my sources?"

"We want that stash pad," the first guy said. "We don't care how you found it."

"Vega just heard about it," I said.

"You're sure?"

"I don't know how long it'll take him to find out where it is, but when he does, the shit's gonna fly."

"That's why we need to get there before he does."

"So you've got one man working on the inside?" I asked.

"He's there in the club right now, but he hasn't had much luck yet."

"I'll take you there. It's about a twenty-minute trip."

"I'm Abrams." The first guy offered me his hand. "My partner's Ross."

I shook their hands. "You got backup you can pull in really quick?"

"Once we locate the site, we can get them in position in ten minutes or less." Abrams pushed open the door. "I'll follow you in my car. Ross, you stay with Deacon."

Ross got out and got back in beside me. As soon as he pulled the door shut, he had his cell in his hand.

"You guys scared the piss out of me in the club," I said.

Ross delivered his text, closed his cell and pocketed it. "Sorry about that, but we couldn't take any chances with the crowd. When you're dealing with Hispanics running a club run owned by Arturo Vega, you really don't know who's listening, and you sure as hell don't know which of the customers are actual customers, and not a direct line to Vega. "

I nodded.

"We had to get you out of there in a hurry. We were afraid you could've blown our investigation."

"So both of you are DEA?"

He nodded.

"And for the last two months, you've been looking for stash pads you can tie in with Vega?"

"Miami's been confiscating close to fifteen percent of what's actually coming in from Mexico and Central America. That's an optimistic estimate, by the way. We think a more accurate amount would be closer to ten. The shipments keep getting bigger coming in, but by the time they leave Orlando, they're much lighter, and when they hit Jacksonville, the amounts reported are even lighter than that."

"You don't think Raguzzo's grabbing any of the stuff?"

"We think Papa Joe's getting his contraband from Bermuda, but he doesn't seem to be that much into drugs anymore. Ever since he had that internal problem last year, his operation's been keeping a low profile. We think the old man's lost his edge and might actually be looking for a replacement. After all, he's pushing seventy-five, and we've heard it from the grapevine that he wants to spend more time on the golf course."

That surprised me. I could tell Papa Joe was getting tired when he'd hired me last year to look for traitors in his organization, but I didn't remember him mentioning a replacement, or spending more time on the golf course.

But I reminded myself that even though Papa Joe considered me a friendly outsider, this didn't mean he'd want to share his inner thoughts with me. The grapevine Ross had just mentioned could be accurate in this case.

"Anyway, we're pretty sure Vega's the one doing the heavy lifting here, so anything you can give us will be appreciated."

"There might be a murder involved," I said. "That's why I've been looking into it. And by the way, this murder involves Heather, the stripper you guys have been trying to shadow."

"How so?"

"As far as I can tell, she's the one pulling the strings and also the one who set up the stash pad in the first place."

Ross shook his head. "Vega's gonna love that."

"If he gets his hands on her, it won't be pretty."

"Neither will she. You got any other info on this murder you just mentioned?"

"The man's name is Daniel Henderson. He's about forty, handles a hedge fund, and runs the firm Henderson & Associates in Orlando. From what I've learned, he was in on it with Heather."

"How accurate is this information?"

"As accurate as it gets without actual photos or recorded conversations. She apparently moved in with Henderson a while back, and no one's seen him for the last three days."

"His business aware of anything funny going on?"

"They didn't say much, but I could tell they're totally in the dark."

"Unless Henderson was dumped somewhere, his body should be showing up eventually."

"There *is* a chance that he isn't really dead…"

"You think that's possible?" Ross asked.

"I have to admit that would be a serious stretch."

"You don't think it's possible that he might be hiding out somewhere?"

"I'm not exactly sure, but I strongly suspect he's out of the picture. I went through his house and didn't find any sign that he'd gone anywhere. His clothes were all there, and there was nothing to indicate a spontaneous trip or absence."

"Find anything at all?"

I pulled out my cell and handed it to him. "I found Heather's stash in her bedroom closet. There's a ton of valuable stuff in there that you guys might be able to use. I'd be careful with the list of names, though. A couple of them could be your bosses. But I have a strong feeling she's been squeezing money from some of them to help finance her trip abroad and probably has enough leverage on them to cause a bunch of sphincters to pucker all the way to Tallahassee. She's got a thumb drive with her stuff. If you happen to come across it, be careful who you show it to."

He took my cell and flicked it on.

"She's flying to Geneva tomorrow evening. She's got three passports, but the one she'll be using will be under the name Gabriella Sanchez. The flight's between ten and eleven tomorrow night."

"I'll notify the airlines." Ross produced his own cell. "And just in case we're busy with this other stuff, I'll contact INTERPOL to make sure she's got a proper reception committee awaiting her arrival."

"What happens when we get to the stash pad, if you don't mind my asking? A raid might not be your best option in this case."

"Once you show us where it is, we'll take it from there. You said Vega knows about it?"

"He just found out."

Ross stared at me. "How'd *you* find out?"

"I've got my sources."

Ross was silent for nearly half a minute before he spoke again. "Haversack told us you had some sort of impeccable inside track, but he didn't go into detail."

"That's only because he doesn't know exactly what my impeccable inside track is."

"I see…"

"When you stumble across something of quality, something you truly value, you don't do or say anything that'll jeopardize the arrangement, no matter what."

Mike smiled.

Ross thought about that for a moment and nodded. "I understand."

"No," I said. "You really don't."

Chapter 17

About twenty minutes later, I crept down the street and passed the stash house, parking in front of someone's Ford pickup six driveways down.

Abrams eased on by, until he reached the end of the block. He parked along the curb across the street, killed his lights, got out quietly and trotted back to the TransAm.

Ross rolled down his window.

"Which house?" Abrams whispered.

"Six down," I said. "The one with the vine-covered trellis."

"There are lights on inside," Ross said, watching.

"No one's there," Mike told me.

"No one's there," I said.

"You're absolutely sure?" Ross asked.

"Paco and Sanchez were there earlier, but they had to go back to work at the club."

"Have any idea if there are sensors or a security system we should worry about?" Abrams asked.

"There's a security system," Mike said. "It's similar to the one at your ex-wife's condo."

"There's a security system," I told them. "I'm pretty sure it's a home security model."

"You wouldn't by any chance have any idea what's in the house right now, would you?" Ross asked.

"Last I heard, there were around a hundred boxes of coke, weed, or both, sitting in the garage.

The boxes are sealed with cellophane and taped, and I believe there's a briefcase with a large amount of money stored in one of the rooms…"

"The master bedroom," Mike said. "It's in the closet—on the top shelf, hidden under some blankets."

"It's in the master bedroom, in the closet," I added. "It's on the top shelf, hidden under some blankets."

They both stared at me. I could clearly feel the confusion.

"You wouldn't by any chance wanna tell us how you know all this, would you?" Ross kept staring at me.

"I've got some pretty reliable sources." I sincerely hoped they wouldn't consider this a problem. It would not only compromise their investigation, it would also jeopardize the seizure of the contraband. Lastly, it would piss me off and discourage me from cooperating with them in the future.

"I'm sure you realize," Abrams said, "that this is looking more and more like you could be a little more involved in this than you're letting on."

"You guys wouldn't be implying that I'm actually in on the action, would you now?"

"The idea occurred to me," Abrams said.

"Me, too," Ross said. "In fact, if Haversack hadn't vouched for you, we'd probably wanna bring you in for questioning."

"I don't believe these two." Mike was beginning to get angry.

"I gave you a stash pad with all the trimmings, and now you're about to screw it up by implying that—"

"We're not gonna screw this up," Abrams said. "We're just a little suspicious about how you know about all this."

"Tell me this... When one of your CI's comes up with some seriously valuable stuff, you're ready to pounce on him as well, right?"

Silence.

"I think you got them with that one." Mike was grinning.

"And you guys wonder why more people don't help out the police," I threw in. "Who would've figured?"

"Haversack said you're clean," Abrams said. "We pulled your file."

"Merely as a precaution, of course," Ross added.

"Find anything exciting in there?"

"Actually, nothing that even remotely suggests corruption," Ross said.

"That's probably because I'm what you might call an honest guy." I was finding it increasingly difficult to control my anger. "You know what that is, don't you? It means I'm not exactly the type who likes breaking the law."

"We did see a couple of notations involving the Raguzzo Organization," Abrams said. "But nothing indicating a possible tie-in."

"Papa Joe and I...well, we have kind of a mutual disrespect for one another. We're both

190

much happier when we give one another his space."

After a short silence, Abrams said, "Still…this seems much too easy…"

"This is ridiculous," Mike said, shaking her head. "Are these two for real?"

"You want the collar or not?"

"Definitely."

"Hell, yeah…"

"Then forget about trying to tie me in on this and concentrate on how you're gonna handle the situation without getting anyone in the neighborhood shot up."

Neither said anything, but I could tell that they both felt like idiots.

"So…what's the plan?" I asked. "I'm sure you don't need me anymore. Actually, I'd prefer it a whole bunch if you don't need me anymore."

"We can't tell you the details for obvious reasons," Ross said. "If you're right about Vega finding out about this, it won't be long before he sends someone here. He's gonna want to get his mitts on his stolen stash as soon as possible."

"It's bound to get ugly," Abrams said.

"I really don't mind getting out of here," I said. I was tired and wanted to go home, have a drink, and sack out for the night. "Just say the word."

Ross nodded. "We should have Federal assistance here within the hour."

"If we're lucky," Abrams said, "we'll be able to wrap this up with minimal casualties." He scanned the deserted street. "At this time of night, traffic should be light. Hopefully, we can haul them all in as soon as they arrive."

"Then my work is done."

Ross opened the door and got out.

"We'll be in touch," Abrams said. "And thanks."

"No problem."

***

Mike and I reached Phil's Winter Park condo a little before midnight.

Phil answered her door wearing a long-sleeve cream crepe blouse, black designer slacks, and open-toed white pumps. The three-inch heels made her an inch or so taller than me, but we'd been through that road before, and anyway, I was much too tired to give her the impression that it bothered me. Besides, she looked fabulous. Her long black hair was tied in a thick ponytail that hung just three inches shy of her waist. As was her custom, she tied it up in the evenings after work and untied it before going to bed.

I noticed right off that she wasn't smoking. To me, this was very strange. Phil normally went through forty or so in a day's time. I smelled the reek on her as always, but she didn't have her usual prop smoldering in her right hand. All I saw was a mug of coffee.

Her large dark-blue eyes, as always, held my gaze, and I could tell she was doing her analytical thing, calibrating what had happened to me in the last twelve hours by taking quick inventory of my face, clothing, and the way I was standing. It had become automatic with her--something she'd learned to do frequently during the years we were together, continuing it long after our ten-year marriage had ended.

Although we would probably never get back together, we remained good friends. But even so, it didn't stop us from our good-natured sparring the moment our eyes met.

"You look tired, Ralph."

"How can you tell?"

A shrug. "The blood-shot eyes, for one thing. And it *is* kind of late—even for you. And, of course, the way you're standing."

"How am I standing?"

"Slightly more stooped than usual. It makes you appear an inch or so shorter."

I immediately straightened. "Where's your cigarette?" I slipped by her and stood in the foyer beside Mike. "You didn't join Hackers Anonymous while I wasn't looking, did you? Or is your velvety skin covered with patches under that breathtaking designer ensemble?"

"You're *such* a funny man." She closed the door behind us and went over to reset the security system. "The smoke was bothering Tabby. I decided to cut down during our visit."

"You...cut down? Seriously?" I was surprised. Phil had never once considered going the cold turkey route during our marriage. She actually enjoyed smoking. I couldn't imagine her giving it up even for a couple of hours, let alone all evening, and noticed how well she was holding up. She wasn't even acting curt, or crabby. "I'm proud of you, Phil."

"It was nothing."

"Really?"

"I don't want to subject an innocent child to second-hand smoke." She finished with the security alarm and turned. I could feel the heat coming out of her eyes. "And please stop the patronizing. It isn't exactly pleasant at this time of day, and I'm not amused or in the mood."

So much for holding up well and not being curt or crabby...

"I don't think you should mention the smoking again," Mike said.

"Right. So...where's the kid?"

Phil gave me one of her deliberate long sighs. It usually meant I'd said something juvenile or insulting. "Once again, her name is *Tabby*, and she's in the kitchen, asleep."

"*Asleep*? In the *kitchen*?"

Phil blinked but said nothing.

"You did say *kitchen*, didn't you? You didn't say guest room or sofa, did you? Closet, maybe?"

"Now why on earth would she be waiting for you in the closet?"

"Maybe she was a bad girl, and you're punishing her for breaking one of your priceless antiques."

Another long sigh. "It's much too late for your kind of humor, Ralph..."

"I don't think you should keep trying to make her laugh," Mike said. "She told you she's not in the mood."

"I think you're right..."

194

Phil glanced at her hand. Frowning at the coffee cup she was holding, she brought it up to her lips and had a sip. She'd apparently substituted caffeine for her nicotine craving. It was obvious since she rarely drank coffee this late. I suspected she wouldn't want to drink her usual quota of white wine while looking after a little girl. Phil had always been the most proper and considerate person I'd ever known. To camouflage the nicotine urge, she'd probably gone through six pots of coffee since she'd come home.

"She wanted to wait up until she heard from you, and when you called, she was so excited, she wanted to be ready, but it turned out to be too late for her. She's had a very long, hard day. She waited and waited, and finally just laid her head down and fell asleep. She's sitting on one of my barstools and hasn't budged in the last fifteen minutes."

"But why is she in the kitchen, rather than the living room? What were you two doing?"

"She was telling me what she'd like to do when she graduates from high school."

"What does she want to do?"

"Art, of course. She'd like to get into graphics or animation--something along those lines."

"Hopefully, she'll go on to study at a good art school when she graduates. Unless, of course, she meets a guy and turns stupid."

"It would be a shame if she didn't pursue it, Ralph. She's really very gifted. And she was very excited when she talked about it. Her eyes got very big and she actually seemed to glow."

Mike and I followed Phil through the living room, down the short hall to the open kitchen area.

Tabby was sitting up at the counter, yawning and rubbing her eyes. When she saw me, her eyes grew and she perked up. "Everything go okay?"

I nodded.

She sat up and pushed a thick clump of red hair out of her eyes. "Did you find my neighbor?"

I sat down beside her. "I've got something to tell you."

Her smile dropped, but her eyes stayed huge. "He's not...not--"

"I'm sorry, Tabby, but Mr. Henderson...well, he got into bad company..."

Phil, the dear, brought me a drink--a shot of Jack's with two cubes. I smiled at her in gratitude and had a sip.

"Please tell me what happened, Deacon..." Tabby's voice had become a whisper.

I put the glass down and stared at it for a few moments, gathering the courage to tell her what she needed to know.

"You'll do fine," Mike said. "Just tell her the truth."

"It's like this, Tabby..."

"*Please* tell me, dammit..."

"All right. But watch your language. Phil, here, gets embarrassed when she hears someone cuss."

Phil sat on a stool across from us and gave me one of her stern looks. "Don't lie to her, Ralph..."

"Here's the story in a nutshell... Your neighbor, like I said--well, he kind of got mixed up with some bad people."

"Was it that blond lady I saw him with?"

"That's right. You saw her, didn't you?"

She nodded. "I told you about her when I first came to your office. I saw her come out of the house with him one Saturday morning. She was a stripper, wasn't she?"

"How could you tell? I got the impression you didn't get a good look at her."

A corner of her mouth turned down. "It was pretty obvious..."

"She's smarter than you think," Mike said.

"She was a stripper, all right."

Tabby was quiet for a few moments. "I think I know what happened, then."

"You do?"

"I know how guys act around strippers."

"The problem was, the man did some really stupid things for her."

"What kind of stupid things?"

"Things he probably wouldn't have done if he hadn't hooked up with her."

"He wasn't stupid, though. He had a business and everything."

"Tabby, people can be brilliant and still do some really stupid things."

She thought about that for a little while. "That sex thing really turns out bad for everyone, doesn't it?"

"Very astute," Phil said.

"Extremely," Mike agreed.

"Yes," I said. "Unfortunately, it's a large part of people's lives."

"That's only because people screw it up, right? Normally, it's a really cool thing."

I nodded. "You're really one special young lady."

Tabby's eyes grew. "You mean...I'm *right*?"

"On the button."

"So can I go home now? I mean, I don't have to worry about those...those scary guys?"

"You'll never have to worry about them again. They're about to be rounded up and brought into the police station. They'll have a lot more to worry about than a little girl who saw them coming out of that house."

Smiling, she held out her arms, reached out for me, and we hugged.

"Thanks, Deacon. Thanks for everything."

"No problem. You need to call your mom and let her know you're coming home."

"We've already done it," Phil said.

"Then...she's not worried?" I asked.

Phil gave me another stern look. I could tell I was in for some immediate scolding. "It took me a little while to figure out exactly what you told the poor girl, but once I got all your lies and excuses sorted out, I talked to Mrs. Kendrick and let her know exactly what was going on."

"She didn't have a coronary?" I asked.

"The lady was very understanding. Of course, she was a little peeved when I told her what you told Tabby to do, but she agreed to be civil to you when you brought her home."

"You were right," Tabby said, hugging me again. "She really *is* a great lady."

"I wouldn't lie about something like that."

She pulled away and stared at me, those big blue eyes probing mine. "Can't you guys…well, can't you at least *talk* about getting back together?"

I glanced at Phil. "It's complicated," I told Tabby.

Tabby frowned. "That's what grownups always say when they don't know what else to say, isn't it?"

Phil nodded. "Yes. *Extremely* astute."

"Look at that." Mike smiled when the kid pressed her face against my chest. "It's so sweet… A true Kodak moment."

"I really should take a picture," Phil said.

That's all I needed--sappy displays of affection from three females in the same room at the same time. The fact that one of them was dead somehow made it even worse.

"Kiddo, do me a favor," I said when she pulled away.

"What's that?"

"Don't be in too much of a hurry to grow up."

"Whaddya mean?"

"You'll turn into just another gorgeous babe with issues, and you'll inflict them all onto some poor schmuck who's got enough troubles of his own. But your schmuck really won't care because he'll be so stuck on you that he won't notice what you're doing to him until it's too late. The bad thing is that by then, he'll be so messed up that he won't know enough to even *care* what's going on, or what you actually did to him."

She blinked. "*Huh*?"

"I honestly hope *I'm* not the one you're talking about," Phil said.

"I was thinking the same thing," Mike said.

Chapter 18

Tabby was quiet on the way back to Oak Ridge Road.

"Talk to her," Mike said from the back. "You need to find out how she really feels about all this."

"You gonna be okay?" I asked Tabby.

She nodded.

"Are you sure?"

"I feel a little weird, but I'll get over it."

"Why do you feel weird?"

"The whole thing's weird. Things started going seriously freaky the night I saw Mr. Henderson disappear right in front of his house. Then they got even worse when those strange guys moved in right after. I really didn't know what was coming off until you took me away so you could hide me. It was all a totally bonkers, ya know? Like one of those detective shows, only it really happened. Life's kinda screwy."

"You're much too young to have already figured that out."

"I figured that out a long time ago."

"When was this?"

"The first time my dad went overseas. Mom was really mad at him for leaving. She stayed that way, and she was totally messed up the whole time he was gone. It was almost like she didn't even see me or anyone else anymore. She was all by herself. She didn't listen to anything I said to her, either, and didn't pay much attention to her job, because they sent her home a couple of times and told her to get a check-up. But when Dad came back, she turned right back to how she was before. Everything was back to normal as soon as he came in the front door. It was just like the eight months he was over there never even happened. Don'tcha think that's kinda creepy?"

"People don't like change, and if they're satisfied with the way things are, they get all spazzed out when something breaks their routine."

She was silent for a few moments. "You really think Mr. Henderson's dead?"

"Probably."

"That sucks."

"It happens."

"All he did was go apeshit over the wrong lady, right?"

"Watch your language."

"Well? Didn't he?"

"Tabby, people die all the time, and a lot of them die because of something stupid."

"I just don't think it's fair."

"Once you realize life isn't fair, that's when you stop being disappointed."

"I just hope my dad comes home okay. He was wounded last time."

"How bad?"

"He said it was shrapnel. It caught him on the leg. He had stitches running all the way down his leg, but he was walking okay."

"He was lucky."

"I just hope he's lucky again."

"I'm sure he'll be all right."

202

"I hope so. He promised us this would be his last deployment."

"Then he has even more of a good reason to make it back in one piece."

Tabby was silent for a little while. Then she said, "What's gonna happen to that stripper?"

"It all depends on what they can nail her with—and if they can grab her before she has the chance to leave the country. They'll probably go after her for her part in the murder of Henderson. If they can tie her in with that, she'll serve life. And as I told you before, don't worry about those men who were at his house. They'll do serious time as well. I'll probably hear about it in the morning. When I find out what happened, I'll give you a call and tell you all about it."

"Will they really tell you? Or is this one of those things they won't talk about unless you're an actual cop? In all those TV shows I've seen, one agency doesn't tell the other one anything, and the bad guys get away because the stupid cops and the Feds are so busy trying to keep everything secret."

"Yeah, they like marking their territory, but I'll get them to tell me."

"How?"

"I have my ways."

"You mean you'll get them all pissed off?"

"You know me all too well, kiddo."

"Why don't you get your friend Mike to find out?"

"Yes," Mike said. "Why don't you do that?"

"What makes you think she can find out any easier than I can?"

Tabby shrugged. "I just have this feeling she can get more done than you can."

Mike smiled. "She's *so* perceptive...and bright...and also *so* right-on..."

"What makes you think that?"

"Didn't you tell me she's a babe?"

"What does that have to do with anything?"

"Babes can usually get what they want a lot easier than guys, right? Isn't that why Mr. Henderson was killed? Because she got him involved with those guys?"

I sighed. "I guess you're certainly right about that..."

"See?" Tabby was grinning. "I *so* totally know what I'm talking about."

"Yes." Mike nodded. "*So* perceptive..."

DAY THREE

Chapter 19

My cell buzzed just a few minutes after I opened up the office the next morning.

It was Neil Haversack, and he didn't sound as surly as the last time I'd talked to him.

"What's happening?" I asked.

"I'm sure you can guess that this place has been hopping since the bust last night."

"A bust? There was a bust?"

"Cut the bullshit, Deacon. You know what I'm talking about."

"Oh, that's right. I guess I scored a point or two with you guys, didn't I?"

A pause. I could tell Neil was trying his best to be cordial—which wasn't easy for him. But he knew he'd better do his best anyway. He couldn't very well treat me badly after I'd just helped the Department close down a stash pad. "Anyway, there were nearly a dozen Latinos at the stash house when DEA rounded them all up, and the bad guys had brought along a truck with them. Apparently they were caught trying to confiscate the contraband when the Feds closed in on them."

"Could you tie Vega in with it?"

"I doubt that's gonna happen. You know these guys won't talk."

"Well, it's definitely gonna piss him off anyway."

"Deacon, that actually turned out pretty damn good..."

I'd known Neil a long time. Although that hardly sounded like a compliment, it was as close to one as I'd ever heard from him.

"You sound surprised."

"I am, actually."

"When have you ever known me not to deliver?"

"You really need to ask me that?"

"I guess I forgot who I was talking to."

"On a serious note, your tip paid off, big-time."

"How utterly refreshing to hear you say such a thing, faithful friend and colleague of so many years."

"Dammit, Deacon..."

"Sorry. Didn't mean to gush. I was overwhelmed. And taken aback. And knocked off-balance. And shocked beyond all--"

"Be serious, now. I just heard back from Kissimmee. This is possibly their biggest haul in months."

"Was it weed?"

"It was high-grade, uncut stuff straight from Colombia. The DEA said they've already gotten with Miami to compare samples of recent shipments. Miami's familiar with the wrappings, and they're pretty sure it's from the Garza cartel. Those boys are responsible for sending fifteen thousand pounds up through Florida every month."

"Any idea where it's going once it gets here?"

"They're pretty sure that by the time it hits Central Florida, as much as twenty percent of the stuff disappears. We think it goes directly to Vega, but we just can't prove it."

"That's a lot more shit than Ross and Abrams told me."

"It's a lot more shit than all of us thought."

"Damn. That's three thousand pounds a month. Slightly more than pocket change."

"They're estimating closer to four, but of course they can't be sure--not enough to make it stick. Kissimmee was working on a lead last month, but they lost contact with their CI a week before the DEA could get hold of him. They figured Vega's people found out and dumped him somewhere, so that put them back at square one. But this really helps. The phones haven't stopped ringing. They're all over this place, badgering us about that anonymous tip."

"I sincerely hope Abrams and Ross didn't tell them anything."

"They're good men. They won't."

"You're sure?"

"I told them you come up with tips like that all the time, so they won't want to cut off their source."

I didn't like the sound of that. "Is that what I am? Their *source*?"

"You're important to them now. Deal with it."

"I'll try."

"Try harder. You don't want the DEA on your ass."

"Any idea how much weed there actually was?"

"Street value hasn't been estimated yet, but from what I heard, it should be substantial. A good night's work for everyone."

"Did they find anything else in the house?"

"They found close to half a mill in a briefcase. Feds figure it was hush money—which usually comes up with each shipment. It's to take care of politicians, troopers, Border Patrol, and anyone else who needs to turn a blind eye. They also figure the amount had been shaved a little, since the stacks registered unequal amounts."

I was pretty sure I knew the lady who did the actual shaving. "Anything else?"

"The print guys haven't finished yet. It should take twenty-four hours for a thorough dusting."

"Nothing obvious?"

"Not much. Whoever was taking care of the place didn't spend much time there. Nothing in the refrigerator or on the shelves. Nothing other than the hidden money in the closets or anywhere else. Just some trash in the can--mostly fast food stuff. They found out who owns the place— owned it, rather."

"Let me guess. Henderson?"

"How'd you know?"

"I just figured Heather Jackson picked her men for specific reasons. Henderson was well-off. He was also good-looking and knew how to dress.

A popular, high-maintenance stripper would need to look at things from a more economical perspective—especially when she was in the process of devising an elaborate scheme of ripping off her boss. And since she was probably looking for a place at the time, Henderson eagerly obliged her. He wanted her and didn't care what it took to get her. She knew about his wealth and his various investments, so he had to make her certain promises to get her in the sack and keep her there. This was exactly what she was looking for, and she knew right then that she had another patsy."

"Henderson owned three houses besides the one he lived in. The other three he'd acquired through fast sales and bankruptcies, but once he'd acquired them, he actually kept them up. They're all being checked out now as we speak."

"So all she had to do was tell him she needed a place, and he jumped at the chance to please her."

"I know a hundred guys who would've done the same damned thing," Neil said.

"Hell, if I was rich and ten years younger, I might've done the same damned thing, too."

"Not many guys wouldn't," he said. "We'll never know if Henderson actually knew what she needed the place for, will we?"

"Judging by how he was suckered outside his home, I'd say he had his suspicions. He probably did or said something they didn't like, so they did him in before he could mess up the works."

"Whatever happened really doesn't matter—not now, anyway."

"What does matter is what happens to Heather," I said. "Any word on that?"

"Seems she just disappeared."

"When did you hear that?"

"Just caught it on the wire as I came in. Apparently after the raid, the DEA went to Henderson's house on Oak Ridge. She wasn't there, and they said it looked like a good portion of her wardrobe was missing. Ross and Abrams checked the stash hole you told them about but found nothing. They were watching all the flights at the airports, again with the help of your intel, but they're pretty sure Vega's men got to her sometime last night and dumped her."

"Well, I can't say as I blame him. She cost the bastard a ton of money, and if any of those men talk—"

"They won't. He's got a staff of attorneys that'll get them out in twenty-four hours."

"Wanna bet they'll never make it to their trial date?"

"I wouldn't bet on any of them surviving two weeks after they've been bailed out."

"Any word on Henderson?"

"It just came in a few minutes ago. Three more DOA's showed up on my screen. The body of one of them had been severely beaten. The face was difficult to identify, but the prints matched Henderson."

"They know what happened?"

"It was made to look like a robbery. The body was found in Kissimmee, behind a warehouse off

192. They think he was probably murdered at least twenty-four hours ago."

"I would've been surprised if he was still alive."

"Once he signed over that property, he was a walking dead man."

"The fairer sex, right?"

"From what I've observed in my forty-odd years," Neil said, "the better-looking a babe is, the colder she is on the inside."

"That's more or less what I've found, too."

"Funny, ain't it? Anyway, thanks again for the tip." *Click*.

I pocketed the cell. Then I went over to the coffeemaker to fix a fresh pot.

Chapter 20

Tabby came to see me a little after lunch that same day.

She walked right in and sat down in the chair facing my desk. I could tell by her serious expression that something was on her mind.

"Everything okay?" I asked.

"I just thought I'd come and see you."

"I see that. Your sudden presence gave you away. Anything wrong?"

"Your ex-wife's really cool."

"Yeah, she's a great lady." When she didn't reply, I said, "Is that why you came all the way over here? To tell me something I already know?"

"She thinks I'm really talented."

"If she thinks that, then you probably are."

"I…just thought she was being nice."

"She never lies about stuff like that. If she didn't think you were talented, she wouldn't have gone on so much about you."

"Is your job the real reason why you two got divorced?"

I shrugged. "I thought I told you all that."

"That was everything?"

"She hated answering the phone in the middle of the night and finding out I was in the hospital. She also hated seeing me coming home with bruises and a bloody nose and lumps on my head. Phil's a very quiet, sensitive person. My job's too violent for her. It made her go on meds for a long time."

212

She shook her head. "You two are totally awesome together."

I didn't reply.

"There's really no chance you'll ever get back together again?"

"Not while I do this for a living…"

She went silent and looked down at her lap. I wondered why she was so interested but decided against asking her about it. The subject wasn't worth debating. Both Phil and I had accepted our new arrangement long ago.

After a few moments she looked up. "Did you ever find out about my neighbor?"

"His body turned up in the morgue."

She took a breath. "Does anyone know who did it?"

"Not yet."

"How about those two guys who were staying at his house?"

"As I told you before, I wouldn't worry about them if I were you."

She was silent for nearly a minute. I could tell she wanted to talk about something else.

"What's wrong?" I asked.

"Something's been really bugging me about all this."

"What's that?"

"This Mike lady who always helps you out…"

I shifted in my seat. "What about her?"

"I never actually saw you talking to her."

"So?"

"I never actually saw you call her, either."

"You were staying with my ex most of the day."

"I know...but something's just not right about it."

"I call Mike whenever I've got something I can't handle myself, and she helps me out. I help her out, too...so what's the problem?"

"Something's just weird about it."

"What could be weird about it?"

She shrugged. "It just *feels* weird..."

"How?"

"It's hard to explain. You don't really have to call her or anything, do you?"

"If I don't call her, how will she know I need her?"

"I dunno. How will she?"

This little girl obviously suspected a lot more than she was telling me.

"You tell me."

"I think I'm kinda weirded out by all those times I caught you making those faces...and saying things...and talking almost like someone was there only you could see..."

"This sounds really interesting," Mike said, drifting into the office. "I hope I showed up in time to hear the juicy bits."

"Mike and I are close, and I already told you why I make those weird faces."

"You said you do it 'cause you're old."

"What's wrong with that?"

"I don't believe you."

"You don't believe I'm old?"

214

"I don't believe you make those faces 'cause you are…"

I nodded but didn't reply.

"There really *is* no Mike, is there?"

"She *is* a lot more perceptive than we thought," Mike said. "Any idea how you're gonna handle this?"

I knew better than nod or even glance at Mike at that moment. I decided right then to tell Tabby what was going on—in a round about way, of course. "Mike died a few years ago."

"Really?"

"Yeah…"

"Sorry. Were you and she close?"

"Very."

"Did you meet her after you and Phil divorced?"

"Of course. I never cheated on Phil."

"How close *were* you and Mike?"

"We were so close that even now I feel almost as if she's still here with me."

"So when you talk to yourself, you're really talking to her, aren't you? Her memory, maybe?"

I nodded.

"It's a way of coping, isn't it? A way of mourning? Remembering her?"

I sighed. "I guess so…"

"I could cry," Mike said, smiling. "I really could just sit down and have a good cry…"

It took all my willpower and self-control to ignore her.

"This is sad," Tabby said.

"You have no idea."

"You miss her, don't you?"

"You have no idea."

"Do you ever go and visit her?"

"Visit her?"

"You know…where she's buried?"

"When I get the urge." I sighed and looked very sad. "But sometimes it's just so…so…you know…"

"I think I do," Tabby said softly, blinking.

"I honestly don't know if I should laugh or cry," Mike said, shaking her head.

If she wasn't dead, I would have slapped her.

**

That evening, after a dinner of Chinese takeout, courtesy of the Chinese restaurant two doors down from my office, I sat on the sofa in the living room of my condo, playing a sloppy version of *"Summertime"* with my harmonica.

I'd been playing the harmonica for some time now but still couldn't manage to get more than a dozen or so tunes right. *"Summertime"* was one of them, although there were a couple of sections in it that came out slightly abysmal. Still, I didn't think I was doing too badly. Besides, it relaxed me, kicking much of the stress I'd endured the last twenty-four hours. I was pleased how the last case had turned out, and even though I'd been forced to give a fourteen-year-old girl some disturbing news, I'd managed to score a point or two with OPD, the DEA, and even the Kissimmee PD. I was also greatly relieved that I hadn't gotten close enough to Vega's operation to put me in harm's way again—as I'd done just a couple of years earlier.

"That wasn't bad." Mike came in through the front door and drifted over to the cocktail table. She hovered above it for a few moments, then lowered herself and sat cross-legged, her nearly transparent elbows resting on her nearly transparent inner thighs. "Very moving, in fact."

"Thank you." I grabbed my drink and had a sip.

"I take it you're in a melancholy mood?"

"Because I'm playing "*Summertime*"?"

"Is *that* what that was? I thought it was something else."

"Don't you have better things to do than criticize my playing?"

"I thought I was complimenting you…"

"Not when you can't even recognize what I was playing."

"Don't go by me. I always get those old songs mixed up."

"I guess it's all right since it was written way before your time."

"Before yours, too."

"My parents got me hooked on all sorts of music when I was a kid. My dad was a jazz buff."

"I already know that. I know about your mom, too. I met her, remember? During our trip down to Lauderdale to see your relatives?"

"I remember. I also remember that you showed up unannounced. It was actually *my* trip—not *ours*. And by the way, you didn't really *meet* my mom. You're dead, remember?"

"How can I forget? You keep reminding me."

"And if I didn't, you'd forget, right?"

"*Touché.*"

I had another sip of Jack. "When Mom was young, she was a flower child. Anything and everything the Beatles did turned her on. She's also a Woodstock nut."

"Mine never seemed to be interested in music."

"That's a shame."

"My grandparents were into jazz."

"I didn't know that."

"My mother liked a lot of the stuff you like."

"I didn't know that."

"They always had the stereo going whenever we went for a visit when I was little."

"You never told me about any of that…"

She shrugged. "It never came up."

"So you actually *have* heard "*Summertime*" before…"

She nodded.

"Cool. Maybe I'll put on Doc Severinsen or Maynard when I'm done with the harmonica."

"Doc's all right, but that screechy Canadian trumpet guy rakes on my nerves."

"I'll try to remember that."

"I think I might have told you that before. So…what have you decided about Tabby?"

"What about her?"

"She almost figured us out."

"But she didn't."

"Next time, we might not be so lucky."

"What do you suggest?"

She shrugged. "I suggest you be more discreet in the future."

"Me? Discreet?"

"You might wanna try a little harder next time…"

"Why?"

"You don't want anyone finding out about us, do you?"

I had another sip of my drink. "I've been really careful since you came into my life, but even so, it's bound to come out one of these days, right?"

"You'll get a reputation."

"What sort of reputation?"

"Word might get out that you're, um, crazy?"

She definitely had a point. Everyone knew I was a smartass and as cynical as they came, but those character flaws generally help a private eye's rep. On the other hand, being crazy would scare away potential customers. "You're right. Something like that could cause a serious blow to my business."

"In other words?"

"I'll be more careful."

"And discreet?"

"That, too…" Sometimes Mike could be a real hard ass.

"You still want me to come to your aid whenever you need me?"

"You have doubts?"

"Just asking."

"Do me a favor."

"What's that?"

"Don't ask about that anymore."

"Whatever you say, kind sir…"

"Good. Now…are you gonna stay for a little while?"

"I guess I can. Why do you ask?"

"I was about to serenade you with another one of my sexy ballads."

"Please do. I promise I'll stay till the very end."

I immediately began my personal rendition of *"Tenderly."*

Mike smiled and began swaying with the music. As soon as I took a breath, she said, "That's really very good. I've always loved *"But Not For Me."*"

I had another belt of Jack and put down the harmonica.

"Why'd you stop?"

"Isn't it about time for you to go off for a recharge?"

Mike looked sheepish. "Did it again, didn't I?"

"Slightly…"

"Oops."

"You won't forget to write, will you?"

"I can't hold a pen."

"Figure of speech."

"I was being clever."

"Is that what that was?"

"What can I say? When you're dead, you have to make do."

"Later, Mike."

"If you wish."

"I wish."

A moment later, she vanished.

I grabbed the harmonica and finished playing *"Tenderly."*

Then I went straight to bed.

OTHER BOOKS BY
DAVID BERARDELLI

THE APPRENTICE
THE WAGON DRIVER
DEMON CHASER
THE FUNNY DETECTIVE
DEMON CHASER II
STEPPING OUT OF MY GRAVE
ESCAPE CLAUSE
FATAL INNOCENCE
JUST A SIMPLE ERRAND
COLORS
WORKING FOR A MOB BOSS
AND DARKNESS FELL
AFTER DARKNESS FELL
DEMON CHASER III
IN ANOTHER REALM
BEYOND RECOGNITION

Titles available through:
Fiction4All